"They left a note."

She handed him a piece of paper, the message on it typed in block letters: YOUR BOY WILL BE SAFE AS LONG AS YOU COOPERATE. YOU AND YOUR BOYFRIEND BRING TEN THOUSAND DOLLARS TO THE ADDRESS WE'LL GIVE YOU TOMORROW AND WE WILL TALK THEN. DO NOT GO TO THE POLICE OR TELL ANYONE ELSE. WE HAVE PEOPLE WATCHING YOU AND WE WILL KNOW. MAKE ONE WRONG MOVE AND YOUR BOY WILL DIE A HORRIBLE DEATH.

Andrea sank into a chair, her hand over her mouth, stifling a sob.

Jack read the note again. "Who is this boyfriend they're talking about?" he asked.

"I don't know. I'm not dating anyone. I haven't, since before my marriage. I think they mean you."

CHRISTMAS KIDNAPPING

CINDI MYERS

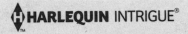

For Jim and Jim

Recycling programs
for this product may
not exist in your area.

ISBN-13: 978-0-373-69943-8

Christmas Kidnapping

Printed in U.S.A.

Cindi Myers is the author of more than fifty novels. When she's not crafting new romance plots, she enjoys skiing, gardening, cooking, crafting and daydreaming. A lover of small-town life, she lives with her husband and two spoiled dogs in the Colorado mountains.

Books by Cindi Myers

Harlequin Intrigue

The Men of Search Team Seven

Colorado Crime Scene
Lawman on the Hunt
Christmas Kidnapping

The Ranger Brigade

The Guardian
Lawman Protection
Colorado Bodyguard
Black Canyon Conspiracy

Rocky Mountain Revenge
Rocky Mountain Rescue

Harlequin Heartwarming

Her Cowboy Soldier
What She'd Do for Love

Visit the Author Profile page at Harlequin.com for more titles.

CAST OF CHARACTERS

Special Agent Jack Prescott—The FBI agent is tortured by the fact that, while he remembers the faces of almost everyone he meets, he can't recall the man who murdered his best friend. His attraction to the therapist he sought help from is complicating his life and distracting him from his duties.

Andrea McNeil—The widow of a cop who was killed in the line of duty, Andrea uses her training as a therapist to help other officers and their families. When terrorists kidnap her son, she turns to one of her patients for help. But the intense and troubled Jack Prescott may be more dangerous to her peaceful, ordered life than she could have imagined.

Ian McNeil—Andrea's son survives a kidnapping and looks up to Jack, but Andrea worries this adoration will only lead to hurt.

Gus Mathers—The fellow FBI agent was Jack's best friend. He was murdered before Jack's eyes, and Jack struggles with guilt and an inability to remember his friend's killer.

Duane Braeswood—The terrorist leader survived a horrific accident and has vowed revenge on the agents who have hounded him. Will Jack be his next victim?

Anderson—The terrorist wants to make a name for himself in the organization. Killing an FBI agent is one way to do so.

Eddie Roland—Braeswood's second in command has taken on more of the lead since his boss's accident, but now agents suspect Roland has a new agenda of his own.

Chapter One

Experience had taught Andrea McNeil to trust her first impressions of a man. She had learned to read temperament and tendencies in the set of his shoulders and the shadows in his eyes. Whether they were heroes or the perpetrators of heinous crimes, they all revealed themselves to her as much by their silences as by what they said.

The man who stood before her now radiated both strength and anxiety in the stubborn set of his broad shoulders and the tight line of his square jaw. He wore his blond hair short and neat, his face clean shaven, his posture military straight, though he was dressed in jeans, hiking boots and a button-down shirt and not a uniform. He moved with the raw sensuality of a hunter, muscular shoulders sliding beneath the soft cotton of his shirt, and when his hazel eyes met hers, she saw pride and courage and deep grief.

"All I want you to do is help me remember the face of the man who killed my friend," he said, before she had even invited him to sit on the sofa across from her chair in her small office just off the main street of Durango, Colorado.

She didn't allow her face to betray alarm at his statement. This certainly wasn't the worst thing she had heard from the people who came to her for help. "Please sit down, Agent Prescott, and I'll tell you a little more about how I work."

FBI special agent Jack Prescott lowered himself gingerly onto the sofa. He grimaced as he shifted his weight. "Is something wrong?" she asked.

"I'm fine."

She kept her gaze steady on him, letting him know she wasn't buying this statement.

He shifted again. "I took a couple of bullets in a firefight a couple of months back," he said. "The cold bothers me a little."

The window behind him showed a gentle snowfall, the remnants from the latest winter storm. A man who had been shot—twice—and was still on medical leave probably ought to be home recuperating, but she might as well have told a man like Jack Prescott that he needed to take up knitting and mahjongg. She didn't have to read the information sheet he had filled out to know that much about him. Even sitting still across from her, he looked poised to leap into action. She would have bet next month's rent that he was armed at the moment and that he had called into his office at least once a day every day of his enforced time off.

Her husband, Preston, had been the same way. All his devotion to duty and reckless courage had gotten him in the end was killed.

She focused on Agent Prescott's paperwork to force the memories back into the locked box where they belonged. Jack Prescott was single, thirty-four years old and a graduate of Columbia with a major in electrical engineering and robotics. Twelve years with the FBI. A letter of commendation. He was in Durango on special assignment and currently on medical leave. He took no medications beyond the antibiotics prescribed for his gunshot wounds, and he had no known allergies. "Tell me about this firefight," she said. "The one in which you were injured."

He sat on the edge of the sofa cushion, gripping his knees. "What happened to me doesn't matter," he said. "But my friend Gus Mathers was killed in that fight. I saw it happen. I saw who killed him."

"That would be traumatic for anyone," she said.

"You don't understand. I saw the man who killed Gus, but I can't remember his face."

"What you're talking about is upsetting, but it's not unusual," she said. "The mind often blocks out the memory of traumatic events as a means of protection."

He leaned forward, his gaze boring into her, his expression fierce. "You don't understand. I don't forget faces. It's what I do, the way some people remember numbers or have perfect pitch."

She set aside the clipboard with the paperwork and leaned toward him, letting him know she was focused completely on him. "I'm not sure I understand," she said.

"I'm what they call a super-recognizer. If I look at someone for even a few seconds, I remember them. I remember supermarket clerks and bus drivers and people I pass on the street. Yet I can't remember the man who murdered my best friend."

"Your talent for remembering faces doesn't exempt you from the usual responses to trauma," she said. "Your memory of the events may come back with time, or it may never return."

He set his jaw, the look of a man who was used to forcing the outcome he desired. "The cop who referred me to you said you could hypnotize me—that that might be a way to get the memory to return."

"I do sometimes use hypnosis in my therapy, but in your case, I don't believe it would work."

"Why not?"

Because there are some things even a will as strong as yours can't make happen, she thought. "Hypnosis requires the subject to relax and surrender to the process," she said. "In order for me to hypnotize you, you would have to trust me and be willing to surrender control of the situation. You aren't a man who is used to surrendering, and you haven't known me long enough to trust me."

"You're saying I'm a control freak."

She smiled at his choice of words. "Your job—your survival and the survival of those who work with you—requires you to control as many variables as possible," she said. "In this case, your need to control is an asset." *Most of the time.*

"I want you to hypnotize me," he said.

"Consciously wanting to be hypnotized and your conscious mind being willing to relax enough to allow that to happen are two different things," she said. "I'm certainly willing to attempt hypnotic therapy at some point, but not on a first visit. It's too soon. Once we have explored the issues that may be causing you to suppress this memory, we may have more success in retrieving it, through hypnosis or by some other means."

He stood and began to pace, a caged tiger—one with a limp that, even agitated, he tried to disguise. "I don't need to talk about my feelings," he said, delivering the words with a sneer. "I don't need therapy. I know the memory of the man who shot Gus is in my head. I just have to find a way to access that information again."

"Agent Prescott, please sit down."

"No. If you can't help me, I won't waste any more of your time."

He turned toward the door. "Please, don't go," she

called. His agitation and real grief touched her. "I'm willing to try things your way. But I don't want you to be disappointed if it doesn't work."

He sat again, tension still radiating from him, but some of the darkness had gone out of his eyes. "What do I do?"

"You don't do anything," she said. "The whole point is to relax and not try to control the situation. Why don't you start by taking off your shoes and lying back on the couch? Get comfortable."

He hesitated, then removed his hiking boots and lined them up neatly at the end of the sofa. He lay back, hands at his sides. His feet hung over one end and his shoulders stretched the width of the cushion. There probably wasn't an ounce of fat on the man, but he had plenty of hard muscle. He wasn't the type you'd want to meet alone in a dark alley, though maybe a dark bedroom...

The thought surprised her, and she felt a rush of heat to her face, glad Jack had his back to her so he couldn't wonder what was making her blush. He folded his arms across his chest, a posture of confrontation and protection. "Put your hands down by your sides," she suggested. "And close your eyes."

"Aren't you going to swing a pendulum or a watch or something in front of my eyes?" he asked.

"That's not the approach I use. I prefer something called progressive relaxation."

"Is that the same as hypnosis?"

"It's a way of readying your body for hypnotic suggestion. Now, close your eyes and focus on your toes."

"My toes?"

"Agent Prescott, if you're going to question every instruction I give, this isn't going to work."

"Sorry. I'll focus on my toes."

"Relax your toes. Now focus on your ankles." She made her voice as low and soothing as possible. "Imagine a warm wave of relaxation moving up your legs, from your toes and feet to your ankles and then your calves and knees. Your body feels very comfortable and heavy, the muscles completely relaxed. The sensation moves up your thighs to your torso. Every bit of tension is leaving your body. Each vertebra of your spine relaxes, one by one. You're feeling very heavy and languid."

She continued the journey up his body, instructing him to relax his shoulders and arms and hands. "How are you feeling?" she asked.

"Fine." His voice was clear and alert, his posture still as stiff as if he were standing for inspection.

"Think of someplace pleasant and relaxing," she said. "A mountain meadow with a waterfall or a beautiful beach with ocean waves rolling in. Choose whatever place you like to go to relax."

"Okay."

"What are you thinking of?" she asked.

"The gym."

She blinked. "The gym?"

"Working out relaxes me."

That explained those impressive shoulders and biceps. "That kind of relaxation is a little too active. What about vacations? Do you like to go to the beach? Or to a lake in the mountains."

"The last vacation I took, Gus and I and some other guys went hiking. We climbed a mountain."

She could imagine—all macho competitiveness: heavy packs, miles logged, not bathing or shaving for days, eating food out of cans. She shuddered. "I don't think this is going to work," she said.

He sat up. "Let's try again. Do the thing with the pendulum. I think I would do better if I had something to focus on."

She hesitated, but if he left here, she would feel she had failed him. She reached up and unclasped the necklace she wore—a gold chain with a gold heart-shaped locket. An anniversary gift from Preston a few months before he died. "Sit back and relax as much as you can," she said.

Jack settled back against the sofa, his gaze fixed on the necklace. "Focus on the heart," she said, and began to gently swing the locket from side to side. "As you focus, count back slowly, from ninety-nine."

"Ninety-nine," he said. "Ninety-eight. Ninety-seven."

She shifted her own gaze from the locket to Jack and found herself staring directly into his gold-green eyes. The naked pain and vulnerability revealed in his gaze startled her so much she almost dropped the necklace. He took her hand. "Please. You have to help me."

His grip was strong and warm but not painful. Far from it. His touch sent warmth coursing through her, as if someone had injected heated platelets into her bloodstream. The heat settled in her lower abdomen, reminding her in a way she hadn't been reminded in many months that she was a woman with a very attractive, virile man touching her. She carefully extricated her hand, which still tingled from the contact. "I want to help you, Agent Prescott," she said. "But the mind is the most complicated machine imaginable. There isn't a formula or solution to solve every problem."

The clock on her desk chimed and she glanced at it. "I'm afraid our session today is over, but I hope you will make an appointment to see me again."

He looked away, frustration clear in the tension along his jaw and the defensive set of his shoulders. "Do you really think it would help me remember Gus's killer?"

"I can't promise you will ever remember what you saw the day your friend was killed," she said. "But I can help you come to terms with what happened."

"Maybe I'll come back," he said.

"I really do think it would help you to talk to someone," she said. "Not only about Gus, but about your own injuries. Being forced into medical leave must be difficult for you."

He looked startled, his eyes locked to hers once more. "The other team members kidded me, said I should enjoy the paid vacation. But it's driving me crazy knowing Gus's killer is out there and I'm not doing anything to help stop him."

"That's something we can talk about the next time you're in." She stood, and he rose also and followed her to the door.

"Do you have another client now?" he asked.

"No, it's time for my lunch break."

He checked his watch, a heavy stainless model she recognized as designed for mountaineers and other outdoorsmen. "Let me take you to lunch. I want to make up for wasting your time this morning."

Her heart sped up at the prospect of being alone with him in a nonclinical setting. "Agent Prescott, I don't think—"

"Call me Jack. And I just want to talk. Not therapy talk, just, you know, conversation. I'm bored out of my skull not working, and I don't know many people in Durango. Not outside of work, anyway. You seem like you'd be good company, that's all."

She should say no. Professional ethics aside— and really, there was nothing unethical about having lunch with a client—spending more time with Jack was dangerous to her equilibrium. He was exactly the type of man who attracted her most—powerful, dedicated, intelligent and virile. And all those traits made him the worst sort of man for her to be with.

But the temptation to sit across from him and learn more of his story, to have his attention fixed on her for a little while longer, won out over common sense. "All right," she said. "I can have lunch with you."

SITTING ACROSS FROM Dr. Andrea McNeil in a café down the street from her office, Jack felt better than he had since the shoot-out. Maybe it was being with a pretty woman. He hadn't dated in a while and she was definitely a looker—her businesslike blue suit did nothing to hide her shapely figure, and her high-heeled boots showed her gorgeous legs to advantage. Her sleek brown hair was piled up on top of her head, drawing attention to the smooth white column of her throat, and she had lively brown eyes above a shapely nose and slightly pouty lips.

But though he could appreciate her beauty, he attributed most of his good mood to the way she focused on him. As if anything he had to say were the most interesting thing she had heard today. That was probably just her therapist's training, but it was doing him a lot of good, so he wasn't going to complain.

"How did you hear about me?" she asked when they had ordered—a salad for her, a chicken sandwich for him.

"I have a friend—Carson Allen, with the Bureau's

resident agency here in Durango. He and I have done some hiking and stuff. Anyway, he said you're the counselor for the police department and the sheriff's office. How did you end up with that job?"

"My husband was a police officer." She focused on buttering a roll from the basket the waitress had brought.

"Was?"

"He was killed three years ago, by a drug dealer who was fleeing the scene of a burglary."

The news that she was a widow—a cop's widow— hit him like a punch in the gut. "I'm sorry," he said. "That must have been tough."

She met his gaze, serene, not a hint of tears. "It was. But I lived through it. I have a son, Ian." She smiled, a look that transformed her face from pretty to breathtaking. "He's five. I had to be strong for him."

"Sounds like he's a pretty lucky little boy." And her husband had been a lucky man. Jack envied his coworkers who had found women who could put up with the demands of a law enforcement job. He had never been that fortunate.

"Tell me more about this talent of yours for re-membering faces," she said. "What did you call it?"

He recognized the shift away from any more per-sonal conversation about her, and he accepted it. "I'm a super-recognizer. I think it's one of those made-up government descriptors the bureaucrats love so much."

"I'll admit I'm unfamiliar with the concept. It must be pretty rare."

He shrugged. "It's not something that comes up in casual conversation. Scientists are just beginning to study facial-recognition abilities. More people may be super-recognizers than we realize. They just don't admit it."

"Why not admit it?" she asked.

"It makes for awkward social situations. You learn pretty quickly not to admit you recognize people you haven't been introduced to. I mean, if I tell someone I remember seeing them at a football game last fall or on the bus last week, they think I'm a spy or a stalker or something."

"I guess that would be strange." She speared a tomato wedge with her fork. "How old were you when you realized you had this talent?"

"Pretty young." For a long time, he had thought that was the way everyone saw the world, as populated by hundreds of individual, distinct people who stayed in his head. "In school it was kind of a neat parlor trick to play on people—go into a store to buy a soda and come out three minutes later and be able to describe everyone who was in there. But as I got older, I stopped telling people about it or showing off."

"Because of the social awkwardness."

"Because it made me different, and if there's anything teenagers don't want to be, it's different."

She laughed, and they waited while the waitress refilled their glasses. "Did your ability get you the job with the Bureau?" she asked. "Or did that come later?"

He shrugged and crunched a chip. "You know the government—they test you for everything. I was doing a different job—one that used my electrical and robotics background—when someone in the Bureau decided to put together a whole unit of people like me and I got tapped for it. Gus was a recognizer, too." A familiar pain gripped his chest at the mention of Gus. Jack didn't have any brothers, but he had felt as close to Gus as he would have any brother. They had been through so much together.

"Is that what brought you two together?" she asked.

"Not at first. We were in the same class at Quantico and we hit it off there. We had probably known each other a year or so before I found out he had the same knack I had for remembering faces. We used to joke about it some, but we never thought anything of it. Not until both of us were recruited for this special project."

"That's really fascinating." She took a bite of her salad and he dug into the chicken sandwich. The silence between them as they ate was comfortable, as if they had known each other a long time, instead of only a few hours.

But after a few more minutes he began to feel uneasy. Not because of anything she was doing. He glanced around them, noting the group of women who sat at a table to their left, shopping bags piled around them. A trio of businessmen occupied a booth near the front window, deep in conversation. A family of tourists, an older couple and two clerks he recognized from the hotel where he had stayed his first two nights in town months ago filled the other tables. Nothing suspicious about any of them. He swiveled his head to take in the bar and gooseflesh rose along his arms when his gaze rested on a guy occupying a stool front and center, directly beneath the flat-screen television that was broadcasting a bowling tournament. Average height, short brown hair, flannel shirt and jeans. Nothing at all remarkable about him, yet Jack was positive he had seen the guy before. Probably only once—repeat exposure strengthened the association. But he had definitely been around this guy at least once before.

"What is it?" Andrea spoke softly. "You've gone all tense. Is something wrong?"

He turned to face her once more. "That guy back there at the bar—the one in the green plaid shirt— he's watching us."

She looked over his shoulder at the guy and frowned. "He has his back to us."

"He's watching us in the bar mirror. It's an old surveillance trick."

"Do you know him?" she asked.

"I've seen him before. Maybe only once. I think he's in our files."

"Why would he be watching you?"

Jack shoved back his chair. "That's what I'm going to ask him."

He pretended to be headed for the men's room, but at the last second, he veered toward the guy at the bar. The guy saw him coming and leaped up. He overturned a table and people started screaming. Jack took off after him, alarmed to see the guy was headed right toward Andrea, who stared, openmouthed. Jack shoved aside a chair and dodged past a waitress with a tray of plates, but his bum leg made speed difficult and the guy was almost to Andrea now.

But the perp didn't lay a hand on her. He raced past, headed toward the door, Jack still in pursuit. Andrea cried out as Jack ran by her. "My purse," she said. "He stole my purse!"

Chapter Two

Andrea stared at the water glass on its side, ice cubes scattered across the cloth. Jack had taken off after the purse snatcher so suddenly she hadn't had time to process everything that had happened. One moment he was saying something about the guy at the bar watching them, and the next her purse had disappeared, and so had Jack.

"Would the gentleman like the rest of his meal boxed to go?"

Andrea blinked up at the waitress, whose face betrayed no emotion beyond boredom, as if purse snatchings and overturned tables were everyday occurrences.

"No thank you," Andrea said. "Just bring the check." She glanced toward the door, hoping to see Jack. Had he caught the thief? Had he been hurt in the attempt? She needed to get out of here and make sure he was okay.

The waitress returned with the check and Andrea

realized that, without her purse, she had no way to pay the bill.

"I'll get that." Jack's hand rested atop hers on the tab. He dropped into the chair beside her, his face flushed and breathing hard. "He got away," he said. "I'm sorry about your purse." He shifted his hip to retrieve his wallet and winced.

"You're hurt," she said, alarmed.

He shook his head. "I'm fine." He removed his credit card and glanced around. Two busboys were righting the overturned table and most of the other diners had returned to their meals. "Where's our waitress?" Jack asked. "I'm ready to get out of here."

He helped her with her coat and kept his hand at her back as they left the café. "What was in your purse?" he asked. "I'm assuming a wallet and credit cards. Driver's license?"

She nodded. "And my car keys, house keys and cell phone." She took a deep breath. "I can call and cancel the cards, get a new license, and I have spare keys at home. I'll have to get a new phone."

"Let me take you by your place to get the keys," he said.

"You don't have to do that. I can call someone." Maybe Chelsea, who was babysitting for her, would come—though that would mean bringing along Ian and Chelsea's baby, Charlotte.

"I have the whole afternoon free, so you might as well let me take you."

"All right. Thank you."

Jack drove a pickup truck, a black-and-silver late-model Ford that was the Western equivalent of a hot sports car. She gave him directions to her home and settled back against the soft leather seats, inhaling the masculine aromas of leather, coffee and Jack Prescott. If some genius were to bottle the combination, it would be a sure bestseller, the epitome of sex appeal.

"Nice place," he said when he pulled into the driveway of the blue-and-white Victorian in one of Durango's quiet older neighborhoods. Snow frosted the low evergreens around the base of the porch and dusted the large pine-and-cedar Christmas wreath she had hung on the front door. Jack had to move Ian's tricycle in order to get to the walkway to the steps.

"Sorry about that," Andrea said. "I keep telling him not to leave it in the way like that, but he forgets."

"He'll be ready for a bicycle before long," Jack said. "If he's five."

"He's been asking for one for Christmas but I don't know..." The thought of her baby riding along the narrow and hilly roads of her neighborhood filled her with visions of collisions with cars or tumbles in loose gravel.

Chelsea opened the door before they were up the steps, Charlotte in her arms. "Oh, hi, Andrea." She sent a curious glance toward Jack. "I didn't know who was here in that truck."

"My purse got stolen at lunch," Andrea said. "I came home to get my spare keys. This is Jack. Jack, this is Chelsea. She's my best friend and she looks after Ian while I work. I don't know what I'd do without her."

"Hello, Jack." Chelsea pushed a corkscrew of black curls behind one ear and smoothed the front of her pink polo shirt.

"I'll just get my keys and get out of your hair." Andrea started to step past her, but at that moment, Ian barreled out of the house.

"Hey, Mom!" He grinned up at her, the dimple on the left side of his mouth and the thick fall of dark hair across his forehead foreshadowing the lady-killer he would no doubt be one day. Just like his father. "You came home early," Ian said.

"Not to stay, I'm afraid." She hugged him and smoothed the hair out of his eyes. But his attention had already shifted to Jack. Ian ducked his head behind her leg and peeked out.

Jack squatted in front of the boy—it had to be an awkward movement, considering his injuries, but a slight wince was the only sign of difficulty he gave. "Hello, Ian," he said. "My name is Jack."

"Mr. Prescott," Andrea corrected. She nudged her son. "Say hello, Ian."

"Hello." The words came out muffled against her

leg, but Ian's eyes remained fixed on Jack, bright with interest.

"What's your favorite food, Ian?" Jack asked.

Ian looked up at his mom. "You can answer him," she said.

"Grilled cheese sandwiches," Ian said.

Chelsea laughed. "He would eat grilled cheese every meal if his mother and I would let him."

"I like grilled cheese, too," Jack said.

"I'll just get my keys." Andrea slipped inside and went to the drawer in her bedroom where she kept her spare set. She paused to study the photo on her dresser, of her and Preston and eighteen-month-old Ian on her lap. Ian liked to hold the picture and ask questions about his father, but one day pictures and her memories weren't going to be enough. A boy needed a father to help him learn to be a man.

She returned to the porch to find Jack and Ian in the driveway, studying something on the tricycle. "What's going on?" she asked Chelsea.

"Guy talk." Chelsea dismissed the two males with a wave of her hand. "What's this about your purse being stolen?" she asked.

"A purse snatcher. Jack chased him, but the guy was too fast." She jingled her keys. "I'll have to call when I get to my office and cancel my credit cards and see about getting a new driver's license."

Chelsea sidled closer and lowered her voice. "Jack

is definitely a hottie," she said. "How long have you two been an item?"

Andrea flushed. "Oh, no, it's not like that. I mean, we just met."

"You don't act like two people who just met." Chelsea grinned.

"I don't know what you're talking about."

"You can't take your eyes off him. And he feels the same way."

Andrea glanced at Jack, something she realized now she had been doing every few seconds since she had returned to the porch. He was kneeling beside the trike, listening while Ian gave some long explanation about something. Just then Jack looked up and his eyes met hers, and she felt a jolt of pleasure course through her.

Jack stood and patted Ian's shoulder. Then the two rejoined the women on the porch. "Ian was telling me about the pedals sticking on his ride," he said. "I'll bring some oil over sometime and fix the problem for him."

"Oh, you don't have to do that," she protested. Jack was a client. They were supposed to have one casual lunch and some conversation. Now he was getting involved in her personal life.

"I'm going to help Jack fix my bike," Ian said.

"Mr. Prescott." Her voice sounded faint, even to her, as she made the automatic correction.

"It's no trouble," Jack said.

Arguing about it, especially in front of Ian and Chelsea, seemed a waste of breath. "All right." She knelt and hugged her son. "I have to give a speech tonight for a police-officer spouse group, so I won't be home until late," she said. "But Chelsea has a special treat for you."

"Pizza and a movie." Chelsea put a hand on the boy's head.

"And root beer?" Ian asked.

Chelsea looked to Andrea. "All right. You may have one glass of root beer with your pizza," Andrea said.

"A big glass," Ian said.

Jack laughed. "You're quite the negotiator, pal," he said.

Ian beamed at the praise. Butterflies battered at Andrea's chest. This wasn't good. She didn't want Ian so focused on a man she hardly knew. Especially a man like Jack, with a dangerous job and a reckless attitude. "We'd better go," she said. "I have clients to see this afternoon."

"I like your truck," Ian said to Jack.

"Maybe I'll give you a ride sometime," Jack said.

Andrea waited until they were in the vehicle and driving away before she spoke, choosing her words carefully. "You shouldn't have said that, about giving him a ride in your truck," she said.

"I would want you to come along, too," he said.

"Saying you'll take him for a ride promises some kind of ongoing relationship."

His knuckles whitened on the steering wheel, the only sign of any emotion. "Would that be so bad?"

She turned toward him, her hands fisted in her lap. "You're my client. I hardly know you."

"I had a good time today," he said. "I'd like to see you again. You and Ian."

"I don't think that would be a good idea."

"Why not?"

"It just…wouldn't."

"Because of the client thing? What if I decided not to see you in a professional capacity anymore?"

"It wouldn't matter." She looked out the window, at the passing lines of shops crowded along the highway in Durango's downtown area. Evergreen garlands, wreaths and hundreds of tiny white lights decorated the Victorian buildings, making the scene look right out of a Christmas card. People filled the sidewalks, hands full of shopping bags, or carrying skis or snowboards, fresh from a day at Durango Mountain Resort.

"Is there someone else?" he asked. "Do you have a boyfriend? I didn't get that vibe from you."

What kind of vibe would that be? But she wasn't going to go there. "I'm busy with my job and raising my son," she said. "I don't have time to date."

"You don't have time to date a cop."

His perceptiveness momentarily silenced her. She stared at him.

"I'm not a trained therapist, but if your husband was killed in the line of duty, it doesn't take a degree to figure out you might not want to repeat the experience." He glanced at her, then back at traffic. "But even civilians can get hit by buses or fall off of mountains or have a heart attack while mowing the lawn."

She shook her head. "I don't want to date you, Jack."

"Fine. But I will have to see you again."

"Why is that?"

"I'm going to try to find out more about the guy who snatched your purse. I'm going to try to find him."

"Don't worry about it. Everything in there can be replaced."

"Maybe. But I don't think he was in that café this afternoon for the sole purpose of stealing a random stranger's purse. He was watching us—watching me—for a while before he made his move. I want to find out why."

"I doubt you'll get my purse back," she said.

"Maybe not. But I have to see you again anyway."

"Why?"

"I promised Ian I'd fix the stiff pedal on his tricycle. And I always keep my promises."

Yes, Jack Prescott would keep his promises. He

would do his duty and live by his pledge, whether that pledge was to a friend or a woman or a little boy like Ian. But he would also keep his promise to give all he had for his country. Even if that meant his life. That last promise was one she wasn't sure she could live with.

AFTER JACK DROPPED Andrea at her office, he called Special Agent Cameron Hsung, one of his fellow Search Team Seven members. "Hey, Jack, how are you doing?" Cameron's cheerful voice greeted him. The half-Asian twentysomething was one of the younger members of the team, an IT specialist who had been recruited, like the other members of Search Team Seven, because of his super-recognizer skills.

"I'm doing great." Jack rubbed his thigh, which burned with pain as a result of his pursuit of the thief and squatting to put himself at eye level with Ian McNeil. "There's no reason I couldn't come back to work right now."

"I'm guessing your doctor has a different idea," Cameron said.

"He says at least two more weeks of leave. But what does he know. How's the case going?" The case—the sole focus of the team at the moment—involved a terrorist cell headquartered here in western Colorado. The suspected leader of the cell, a man named Duane Braeswood, had jumped from the Durango and Silverton tourist railroad two months ago, but a subsequent search hadn't turned up his body.

"We got a lead that a man matching Braeswood's description had shown up at a hospital in Grand Junction," Cameron said. "But by the time local law enforcement made it there, he had disappeared."

"So he was injured?"

"Pretty badly, I guess," Cameron said. "After a bit of a hassle, we got a copy of the medical report. He had a broken leg, some busted ribs, and a bruised liver and kidneys."

Jack winced. "So he probably didn't get to the hospital—or out of it—on his own."

"That's what we're thinking. We got some security video but it's pretty blurred. Typical cheap system that hasn't been maintained. Nobody thinks about these things until they actually need the equipment to do its job. Then it's too late."

"The man doesn't seem to have any shortage of helpers," Jack said.

"Yeah, well, money buys a lot of things—even friends."

"Right. And speaking of friends, I need a favor."

Cameron groaned. "Something tells me I should say no before I even hear this."

"It's nothing complicated. A friend of mine had her purse stolen while we were at lunch today."

"You have a woman friend?"

"Don't act so surprised."

"At least you're using your leave productively. Who is she? How did you meet?"

"Her name is Andrea McNeil. She's a therapist."

"You mean the police therapist you were going to see? Man, what did you do, put the moves on her from the couch?"

"We were having lunch. That's all." Though he definitely wanted more. A guy didn't meet a woman like Andrea every day, and he wasn't buying her argument that she didn't want to date him. He understood her reluctance, given her history, but she must have felt the connection between them. And he thought he was savvy enough to have picked up that she hadn't agreed to have lunch with him because she fell for his "I'm so lonely" line. She was really interested. All he had to do was take it slow and prove that exploring the chemistry between them was worth the risk. "I thought I recognized the purse snatcher. I think he's in our database."

"Uh-huh. And what is this favor you want from me?"

"I want a copy of the database so I can look for this lowlife and find him."

"That database is classified," Cameron said. "It's not supposed to leave this office."

"It's not like you're releasing it to a civilian. I'm a member of your team."

"Technically, you're not on the team right now.

You're on medical leave. You're not even allowed to come to the office."

"Because some bureaucratic pencil pusher is afraid of getting sued if I slip and fall on a wet floor or something before my doctor has cleared me to return to work. That's why I need a copy of the database on my personal computer."

"Jack, it'll cost me my job if anyone finds out."

"No one will find out. It's not like I'm going to go around showing the thing off. I just want to track down this guy."

He thought he heard Cameron's teeth grinding together. "All right. But don't go all Lone Ranger on me. If you find anything, you bring it to us."

"I will. I promise."

"Okay. Meet me when I get off at six, at that tavern around the corner."

"The Rusty Moose."

"Yeah. Dumb name, good beer. You can buy me one and I'll get you what you need. And hey, if your therapist friend has a friend, maybe you could introduce us."

"You have to find your own dates, Cam. That's where I draw the line."

"Hey, I figured it was worth a try."

Jack hung up the phone and started the truck. He couldn't shake the feeling the purse snatcher had been up to more than looking to steal a handbag. There had to be a connection to his case. Even if he was supposed to be on medical leave, that didn't mean he couldn't do a little investigating on his own. He was out of the hospital and doing pretty good. He had never been the type to sit around and do nothing, and he wasn't about to start now.

BY THE TIME Andrea made it home from her meeting, she was drained. As much as she enjoyed sharing her expertise with groups, she identified a little too closely with the challenges faced by members of the Law Enforcement Spouses organization. She remembered what it was like to be in their shoes and deal with the constant worry about her loved one. Though she was happy to listen to their concerns and offer strategies for coping, she knew her words weren't really enough.

She was surprised to find the house dark when she arrived. Chelsea usually left the porch light on for her. She fumbled her way up the steps and opened the door. Silence greeted her—another oddity. Even though it was past Ian's bedtime, Chelsea liked to stay up and watch movies or her favorite reality TV shows. "Chelsea? Is everything okay?" she called as she reached for the light switch.

A half-eaten pizza sat on the coffee table, an almost-empty glass of root beer tipped on its side next to the pizza box, the brown liquid pooling on the table and dripping on the floor. One of the couch pillows was on the floor, too. Heart in her throat, Andrea took a step forward. Then she saw the blood.

Or at least, she thought it was blood. The pool of brownish-red liquid on the rug beside the coffee table definitely wasn't root beer. It could have been spilled syrup, except that no one would be eating syrup with pizza, would they?

She reached for her phone to call 911, but of course, the thief had stolen it, along with her purse. "Chelsea!" she shouted, headed toward the kitchen and the phone there. "Ian!"

She stumbled over something in the hallway—Chelsea lay on her back, her hands and feet tied, a gag in her mouth. She stared up at Andrea, eyes wide. Shaking, Andrea dropped to her knees and pulled the gag from the babysitter's mouth. "What happened?" she demanded. "Where is Ian?"

"Ian's gone." Tears spilled out of Chelsea's frightened eyes. "Two men took him. He's gone."

Chapter Three

Jack spent most of his evening stretched out in the recliner in his apartment, his laptop propped on his stomach, scanning the database Cameron had loaded onto a flash drive. A football game on the TV played in the background, and he was debating getting out of the chair and hunting in the refrigerator for a beer when his cell phone rang. He didn't recognize the number on the screen, though it was a local exchange, and he almost let the call go to voice mail but decided to take a chance. "Hello?"

"Jack, they've taken Ian. You've got to help me. Please. They've taken my baby."

He didn't recognize the voice of the hysterical woman on the other end of the line, but the name Ian meant it had to be Andrea. "Andrea? Is that you?"

"Yes. Oh, God—Jack. Ian will be terrified. You have to help me find him."

"I'll be there in five minutes." He was already moving toward the door. "Can you sit tight until then?"

"Yes. But hurry, please."

He broke several traffic laws on the way to Andrea's house, but traffic was light off the highway this time of evening, and in less than five minutes he roared into her driveway. Every light in the house was illuminated. He raced onto the porch and knocked. "Andrea! It's me, Jack."

"Come in. We're in the kitchen."

He found her at the back of the house, applying a cold washcloth to a nasty-looking bruise near the babysitter's temple. Chelsea held her baby close, tears pouring from her eyes as she rocked and cooed at the infant. Andrea had been crying, too, her eyes red and swollen, cheeks streaked with tears. "What's going on?" Jack asked.

"Ian and I were watching a movie and eating pizza and these two men dressed in black and carrying big guns burst in and grabbed him," Chelsea said. "I tried to stop them, but one of them hit me in the head with the butt of the gun. When I woke up, I was tied up and gagged in a back bedroom and Ian was gone." She gulped and swallowed hard. "I was so afraid they'd taken Charlotte, too, but they left her sleeping in her crib."

"Have you called the police?" Jack asked.

"They said not to," Andrea said. "They said they would kill Ian if I contacted any law enforcement." Her voice wobbled at the word *kill* and she looked ready to collapse.

Jack put his hand on her shoulder to steady her. "Who told you not to?" he asked.

"I don't know who. They left a note."

She handed him a piece of paper, the message on it typed in block letters.

YOUR BOY WILL BE SAFE AS LONG AS YOU COOPER-ATE. YOU AND YOUR BOYFRIEND BRING TEN THOU-SAND DOLLARS TO THE ADDRESS WE'LL GIVE YOU TOMORROW AND WE WILL TALK THEN. DO NOT GO TO THE POLICE OR TELL ANYONE ELSE. WE HAVE PEOPLE WATCHING YOU AND WE WILL KNOW. MAKE ONE WRONG MOVE AND YOUR BOY WILL DIE A HOR-RIBLE DEATH.

Andrea sank into a chair, her hand over her mouth, stifling a sob. Chelsea leaned over and squeezed her hand.

Jack read the note again. "Who is this boyfriend they're talking about?" he asked.

"I don't know. I'm not dating anyone. I haven't since before my marriage."

"I think they mean you," Chelsea said.

"Me?"

"Jack isn't my boyfriend," Andrea protested.

"If the kidnappers saw the two of you together this afternoon, they might think so," Chelsea said. "I mean, I did."

Andrea moaned and covered her mouth again.

Jack sat across from her. His leg throbbed, but he

ignored it. "The only person watching us this afternoon was that guy in the restaurant," he said.

"Did you find out who he is?" Andrea asked.

He shook his head. "I'm still looking into it." He glanced around the room. "He probably got your address from your license in your purse. And he has your keys, too." Why hadn't he thought of that before? He should have made Andrea change her locks. Or he should have insisted on staying here at her house tonight. He turned to Chelsea. She looked as wrecked as Andrea, clutching the child in her arms so tightly it was a wonder the infant didn't wail. "What did these two look like?" he asked.

She shook her head. "They were wearing masks, dressed all in black. They carried big guns. Everything happened so fast..."

"How tall were they? How much did they weigh? Did they have accents? Could you see their hands, get an idea of race?" He knew he sounded like a bully, firing questions at the upset woman, but he couldn't help himself. In situations like this, gathering as much evidence as possible as quickly as possible could make the difference between life and death.

Fresh tears spilled from Chelsea's eyes and she shook her head again. "I'm sorry. I don't know. I was so focused on Ian and the guns. And then they hit me." She began to sob, and Andrea pulled her close.

"Why would someone do something like this?"

Andrea asked. "How did they know I had a child? Have they been following me for a while now?"

Jack considered the questions. "This doesn't make sense as a kidnapping." He tapped the note. "For one thing, the ransom is too low. Kidnappers ask for millions of dollars, not a few thousand."

"They must have known I don't have millions," Andrea said.

"Maybe this doesn't have anything to do with you," Chelsea said. "Maybe they got their houses mixed up. You see that on TV sometimes. What do they call them—home invasions."

"Maybe." Jack reread the note. "But I don't think so. How long would you say they were in the house?"

Chelsea frowned, concentrating. "I don't know. They burst in and knocked me out right away. They were here long enough to tie me up and put me in the bathroom. After I woke up, I spent a half hour or more crawling down the hall, trying to get to the phone."

"It sounds to me as if this was planned," Jack said. "They came in fast and hard, took out Chelsea, grabbed the boy and left. They didn't kill Chelsea, though they easily could have, and they left her baby alone. They wanted Ian." His eyes met Andrea's. "And they wanted you to cooperate. They knew taking your son would make you do whatever they wanted."

"But why me?" she asked. "I've never hurt anyone in my life."

"Your husband was a cop," Jack said. "Maybe he made enemies. It could be someone he put in prison. They're out now and seeking revenge."

"Preston has been dead three years. Anything they do to me or Ian now doesn't touch him. These people would be taking a lot of risk for nothing."

He nodded. While he'd learned not to discount some people's drive for revenge or the irrational ways evil people could act, this didn't feel like that kind of situation. The note hadn't mentioned Andrea's husband at all.

But it had mentioned her "boyfriend." "Maybe whoever did this was trying to get to me," he said.

"To you?" Confusion clouded her eyes. "But, Jack, I hardly know you. We just met."

"I can't prove it yet, but I think the man I saw in the restaurant this afternoon is connected to a case I've been working on. He may have seen the two of us together and assumed a relationship. He stole your purse in order to learn where you live. He may even have meant to kidnap you and send the ransom note to me, but when they found Ian instead, they decided to use him."

"That's crazy," Chelsea said.

"It is. But this group has done this kind of thing before." Months before, Duane Braeswood and his men had kidnapped the sister of a woman who worked for the head of the Senate Committee on Homeland Security. They had threatened to kill the sister if the woman, Leah Carlisle, didn't cooperate with them. Once Leah was in their power, they had killed her sister and held Leah hostage for six months. Search Team Seven had rescued her in the same raid in which Gus had been killed. "They know that most people will do almost anything to save their loved ones, more than they would do, even, to save themselves."

"But I'm not your loved one," Andrea said. "I'm just an acquaintance you had lunch with."

"No. But I'm not going to turn my back on you when you need my help." And he cared about her. And Ian, too. In the short time he had known them, they had worked their way into a corner of his heart.

She looked away. "I don't have anyone else I can call," she said. "Not anyone who would be safe. If you can pretend to be my boyfriend until we get through this…" She let her voice trail away, as if she thought she were asking too much.

"I'm not going to leave your side until we're through this." He gripped her shoulder again. "You've got to be strong now. For Ian."

She sat up straighter and took a ragged breath. "What do we do now?" she asked.

"Can you get ten thousand dollars together?"

"I can take it out of my savings as soon as the bank opens in the morning."

"Let's wait until the kidnappers call with instructions. Right now, you can't stay here tonight."

"No." She hugged her arms across her chest and shivered.

He turned to Chelsea. "What about you?"

"I want to go home to my husband. I haven't told him about any of this yet. I'd rather do it face-to-face."

"He'll want to call the police." Andrea clutched Chelsea's hand. "You have to convince him to keep quiet."

"I will," Chelsea said. "He won't like it, but he won't want anything to happen to Ian, either."

Jack stood and walked to the phone on the wall. "What are you doing?' Andrea asked. "Who are you calling?"

"I'm forwarding this number to my cell phone. That way you can come with me and we won't miss a call from the kidnappers."

"The note says they have someone watching me," Andrea said. "Maybe we shouldn't leave the house."

"They think I'm your boyfriend. They won't be alarmed if you come with me." At least, he hoped that was the case.

Andrea packed an overnight bag and Chelsea retrieved the baby's car seat from her vehicle. "My husband can bring me by to get my car later," she said. "I'm too scared to drive home alone right now."

"I don't mind taking you home. And I'll talk to your husband, too. I'll persuade him to keep quiet."

Chelsea's husband turned out to be a burly mechanic who worked for the local Ford dealer. He listened to the story Chelsea told with growing signs of alarm. When she got to the part about needing to keep quiet, he started shaking his head.

Jack stepped forward. "Mr. Green, I'm with the FBI," he said. He opened his ID folder to show his badge and credentials. "I'm going to be doing everything I can to get Ian back to his mother safely, and for that, I need your cooperation."

"FBI!" Chelsea gasped. "Andrea, you didn't tell me he was a fed."

Andrea said nothing, her face pale and drawn. She looked as if the slightest breeze might make her collapse. Jack resisted the urge to gather her close and hold her tightly. "Will you promise not to contact police and not to say anything to anyone—coworkers, friends, relatives, anyone—until this is resolved?" he asked.

Mr. Green nodded. "Sure. I'll keep quiet. I didn't know the FBI was involved."

Not officially, Jack thought. *Not yet.*

They drove in silence to his apartment. Andrea made no protest when he took her arm and guided her up the stairs to the furnished unit he had rented when the team relocated to Durango the month before. The television still broadcast the ball game, the sound turned down low, and the harsh overhead light illuminated the wrappings from the sub sandwich and chips that had been his dinner.

"The bedroom is back this way," he said, steering her toward the short hallway that led to the unit's single bedroom and adjoining bathroom. "You can sleep here. I'll take the couch."

Covers spilled onto the floor, silent testimony to a restless night. The pillow still bore the imprint of his head. He rushed forward to jerk the comforter into place. "I'll get some clean sheets," he said, moving past her.

"You don't have to go to all this trouble," she said, her hand on his arm. "I can take the sofa."

"No, it's okay."

He found the sheets, and together they made the bed, an ordinary, intimate activity that broke some of the tension between them. "Do you have a washer and dryer?" she asked, gathering up the old linens. "I can wash these."

"I'll get them later." He took the mound of sheets from her and stuffed them into the closet behind him. "Can I get you anything else? Tea? Bourbon?"

A smile flickered across her lips. "The latter is tempting, but I want to keep a clear head."

"Try to get some sleep." He hesitated, then reached out and squeezed her shoulder. She leaned her cheek against his hand, her skin silky and warm, and no man with feelings would have been able to resist pulling her to him.

She welcomed the gesture and snuggled against him, her head buried in the hollow of his shoulder. "I'm so afraid," she whispered. "If they hurt Ian…"

"Shh." He cradled the back of her head, his fingers threaded through her hair, which was coming loose from the pins that held it atop her head. He removed the pins one by one and combed out her locks with his fingers. She sighed and settled against him more firmly, so that he was aware of the soft weight of her breasts against his chest and the vanilla-and-honey perfume of her hair. He wanted to bury his face in those silky tresses—and bury the rest of himself in her, as well.

She raised her head and tilted her face up to his, her expression questioning. "Why do I feel so safe and comfortable with you?" she asked.

"Because you are safe with me." He stroked her cheek, silken and warm. "I'm not going to do anything to hurt you."

"Kiss me." She whispered the words, but they had the force of a command. One he was all too ready to obey.

Her lips were as soft and supple as he had imagined, and she responded to the gentle pressure of his mouth by rising up on her toes and angling her head to deepen the contact. This was no meek surrender to his will, but the urgent encouragement of a partner who wasn't afraid to take the lead. She traced her tongue along his bottom lip and he opened to her and shifted to snug her body between his thighs, letting her feel how much he wanted her.

She was the first to break contact, looking up at him with heavy-lidded eyes. "That was as amazing as I thought it might be," she said. "Thank you."

"I'm the one who should be thanking you."

She gently moved out of his embrace. "That was very selfish of me," she said. "I was feeling so helpless and lost… I thought if I kissed you then, just for a moment, I could forget how terrible everything is."

He rubbed his hand up and down her upper arm, as much to avoid breaking contact with her as to comfort her. "Did it help?"

Her eyes met his, the desire he'd seen there only a moment before edged out by sadness. "It did. But it doesn't change our situation." She stepped back, putting space between them. "I'm not trying to lead you on. I think I'm so stressed and upset, and I've been on my own so long…" She shook her head. "It's like my emotions have gone all haywire."

"You don't have to apologize for anything." He understood her more than she would probably believe. The combination of stress and many months of living alone had no doubt intensified his desire for her, but that didn't explain the tenderness beneath the lust, and the fierce desire to make things right for her. He wanted to return her son safely to her, and he wanted to see her smiling and happy again.

"We're going to find Ian," he said. "Hold on to that thought." He turned away. "Try to get some sleep." All he wanted was to crawl into that bed with her and hold her all night long, but she'd probably misinterpret his actions, think he was taking advantage of her vulnerability. If he was going to help her, she had to trust him, and that meant letting her dictate the pace of their relationship. So, while he wanted to stay, he made himself leave the room and shut the door quietly behind him.

ANDREA DIDN'T KNOW how long she stood where Jack left her, clinging to the memory of his warmth and strength. How long had it been since a man had touched her with such tenderness? She had savored the feeling, even as shame lurked in the background, mocking her for enjoying even a minute while her son was in danger. But she'd needed those few moments in Jack's arms to pull herself together and to gather her own strength to keep from breaking down. Though the urge to collapse onto the bed and give in to the sobs that pressed at the back of her throat almost overwhelmed her, doing so wouldn't bring Ian back to her.

She went into the bathroom and washed her face and brushed her teeth, then returned to the bedroom and contemplated the freshly made bed. No way would she sleep tonight, not with thoughts of her boy, frightened and with strangers, haunting her.

She went into the living room and found Jack seated on the sofa, a laptop opened on the table in front of him. He had turned off the TV and a cup of coffee steamed at his right hand. He looked up when she moved into the light. "I couldn't sleep," she said, and sat beside him.

"I figure we're both in for a long night," he said. "Would you like some coffee? I just made it."

"Maybe in a minute." She nodded to the laptop. "Are you looking for the purse snatcher?"

"Yes." He shrank the screen and picked up the coffee cup. "No luck so far, but I'm just getting started."

"I don't mean to keep you from your work." She sat back and grabbed a small throw pillow to hug across her stomach. "I promise not to look."

"I'll take a break for a few minutes." He sipped the coffee and neither of them said anything for a long moment. The refrigerator hummed in the small kitchen behind her, and somewhere below, a car door slammed.

"Why did you call me tonight?" he asked.

A reasonable question, but one she wasn't sure she could answer. "I don't know. I wasn't even thinking. I guess...you're an FBI agent. And you knew Ian. Or at least, you met him and talked to him." She looked at him, the truth of her next words making her a little shaky. "I believed you could save him." But why would she believe such a thing about a man she scarcely knew? Still, she couldn't shake the conviction that if anyone could help her, it was Jack. The stubbornness and commitment and need for control that had struck her as negative traits in her office now stood out as exactly the characteristics needed to fight the evil responsible for her son's disappearance.

"I'll do everything I can to get him back to you," he said.

She forced herself to stand on shaky legs. "I think I'll have some of that coffee now."

When she returned from the kitchen, he was focused on the computer once more. She moved around the room, then studied the few books on a shelf by the door—an acclaimed biography of Theodore Roosevelt, a guide to Colorado's Weminuche Wilderness, a few thriller novels and a thick treatise on the history of terrorism. A single photograph graced the shelf by the books: two men, dressed in hiking gear and standing side by side atop a mountain, beaming at the camera. If she had to guess, she would say the man next to Jack in the photo was his friend Gus, the one whose death tormented him.

"I think I've got something," Jack said.

She hurried to the sofa, scooting close to him to study the picture on the computer screen. A man looked back at her from a grainy black-and-white photo. "It's from a surveillance camera," Jack said.

"Not the best quality, but good enough I can recognize him. This is the guy in the restaurant—the one who stole your purse."

She leaned forward and squinted at the image. It was of a white man, fairly young, with light brown hair and a sharp nose. But nothing about him looked familiar. She shook her head. "I don't recognize him. But I wasn't really paying attention in the restaurant and his back was to me."

"That's all right," Jack said. "I got a good look at him and this is the guy." He clicked to the next screen and she read the name there. Anderson.

"Is that a first or a last name?" she asked.

"We don't know." Jack scanned the few lines of information under the name. "We don't know a lot, but we suspect he's connected to a terrorist cell we've been tracking here in Colorado."

"Terrorists? You think Ian has been kidnapped by terrorists?" The knowledge refused to sink in. What would terrorists want with her little boy? Tears stung her eyes. Where was Ian now? What were they doing to him? If they hurt him...

Jack gripped her hand, pulling her back from the nightmare of horror she was capable of imagining. "We're going to find them, and we're going to get Ian back," he said.

She nodded, struggling for control. "Yes." That belief was the only life preserver she had. "We're going to get him back."

Jack turned to stare at the picture on the computer screen once more, and when he spoke, his voice was colder and harder than she had imagined it could be. "Tomorrow Anderson and his friends will be sorry they ever messed with me."

Chapter Four

The call came at 6:13 a.m., forwarded from Andrea's home phone to Jack's cell. He sat up on the sofa, where he'd fallen into an exhausted doze sometime after three, and snatched up the phone as the last notes of "What It's Like" sounded. "Hello?"

"Agent Prescott. Are you alone?"

The voice wasn't familiar, and the echoing quality of it made Jack suspect it was being filtered electronically to disguise it. "Andrea is here with me, but no one else."

"Good. Let me talk to Dr. McNeil."

Andrea was already standing in the doorway to the bedroom, staring at him with equal parts hope and dread. Jack held the phone out to her. "It's him. Or somebody with him."

She pressed the phone to her ear, clutching it with both hands. "Hello? Is Ian all right? Please let me speak to Ian."

"Your son is safe. For now. Do you have the money we asked for?"

"I'm going to the bank to get it as soon as they open. I don't keep that kind of cash in the house."

"That's fine. You haven't told anyone about what happened?"

"Only Jack. And my babysitter and her husband know, but only because she was there when he was taken. She doesn't remember much and we made them both swear not to tell." The words came in a rush, all her anxiety translated to speech. She wanted these men to know she was cooperating with them. She would do anything to see her son safe.

"Good. I'm going to give you an address. Write this down."

"Hold on. I need paper and a pen." She motioned and Jack thrust a notepad and pen into her hand. She copied down the address the man dictated and read it back to him. "Where is this?" she asked. "It doesn't sound like Durango."

"It isn't. But I'm sure you can find it. Bring the money to this address by noon today. Agent Prescott can come with you, but no one else. If we even suspect police or FBI or anyone else is around, we'll slit Ian's throat and let him bleed to death right in front of you." He ended the call.

Andrea sank to the floor, her legs no longer able to support her. Jack lowered himself beside her and pulled her close. "I heard," he said. "He's trying to intimidate and frighten you."

"It's working." She covered her mouth with her hand in a vain attempt to stifle her sobs. "My poor baby."

Jack let her cry for a minute or so. Then he held her away from him and shook her gently. "Come on. We've got work to do. We're going to get Ian back today. Focus on that."

She nodded and sucked in a shaky breath. "Okay. What do we need to do?"

"Take a shower and get dressed. I'll make more coffee. Then we'll plan our strategy."

When Andrea emerged from the bedroom fifteen minutes later, showered and wearing fresh clothes, Jack handed her a cup of black coffee. "I've decided I should go by myself to meet these people," he said. "This smells of a trap and there's no need to put you in danger when I'm the one they really want."

"My son is in danger. There's no way I'm not going with you to get him." Her eyes blazed and her face had taken on some color for the first time in hours.

He hadn't really thought he could convince her to stay behind, but he felt he had to try. He nodded and picked up a gun from the kitchen table and handed it to her. "Then you'll need this." She stared at the compact weapon, matte black and deadly looking.

"It's a Beretta Storm," he said, pulling the slide back to reveal an empty chamber. "Nine millimeter, double- or single-action trigger, ambidextrous safety." He placed the gun in her hand. "Do you know how to shoot?"

She nodded. "Preston took me to the range and made sure I was competent."

"Good." He nodded toward the box of ammo on the table. "Load it, and be ready to use it if you have to, though I hope you don't have to."

He pulled out his Glock and checked the load. The last time he had fired the weapon was the day Gus died.

"Preston had a Glock like that," she said. "I still have it in the gun safe at home."

He holstered the weapon again. "We could be walking into a trap," he said. "We're going to have to be on our guard."

She nodded. "We have to find the address first."

He picked up the notepad with the scrawled address and walked to the laptop on the coffee table. A few minutes of searching online and he came up with a location. "It's about twenty-five miles out of town, near the community of Bayfield. Do you know it?"

She sat next to him and laid the now-loaded weapon beside the computer, the barrel facing away from them. "I've driven through it a few times. From what I remember, there isn't much there—a few houses, maybe a gas station. I guess the kidnappers chose it because it's remote and probably not very busy this time of year."

"Let's see if we can get a look at it." He pulled up

Google Earth and keyed in the address. By zooming in and maneuvering the mouse, he was able to get a bird's-eye view of a cluster of buildings alongside a river. "Pine River," he read. "This address looks like a fishing camp."

He switched to Street View and studied the image of what appeared to be boarded up buildings. The image had been captured in the summer and showed a dirt road leading into the property, and the surrounding woods. "It's a pretty good setup," he said. "The river protects them on one side and there are dense stands of trees on the other sides. It's well hidden from the road, and from the looks of the place, no one has lived there for years."

"If we drive in there, we'll be trapped," she said.

"We're not going to drive," he said. "At least, not right away. We're going to park some distance away and hike in cross-country. And we're going to do it long before noon. I want a look at this place and whoever is there before they expect us."

"I just realized the man on the phone referred to you as Agent Prescott. How did he know your name?"

"Because I'm the one they're really after." He looked at her. "If things go bad out there, I want you to take Ian and run, as far and as fast as you can. Don't worry about me."

Her eyes shone with tears and her face was the

color of paper. She nodded. "I don't want to leave you," she said. "But I have to save Ian."

"We'll need to dress warm, with good boots and warm coats, hats and gloves," he said. "We can swing by your house on the way to the bank and get what you need. The weather forecast is calling for a major storm cell to move into the area by afternoon."

"The bank opens at nine," she said. "If we leave here at eight thirty, we can go to my house, then the bank, and leave from there. I can change shoes in the truck on the way down."

Now that the pressure was on, she had pulled herself together and was all business. "You would have made a good cop," he said.

Her expressive face revealed anger and pain. "I know you probably mean that as a compliment," she said. "But I don't see it that way." She picked up the gun again and stood. "I'll be ready to go when you are."

THE FIRST FLAKES of snow began to fall as they moved away from Jack's truck. They had parked the vehicle off the road, hidden by a thick stand of juniper, to the west of the fishing camp. It had taken almost an hour to reach the camp from Durango, the last thirty minutes on a winding snow-packed road that crossed and recrossed the Pine River. "We've got to hike about two miles," Jack said. "We'll have to find a place where we can watch the camp without being seen."

Andrea pulled down the knit cap on her head and checked that the gun was secure at the small of her back beneath her winter coat. She hoped she wouldn't have to fire it, but she would if it meant saving Ian. "I'm ready," she said.

Jack led the way into the snowy woodland. He moved swiftly but silently, sinking to his shins in snow with each step. Andrea tried to follow in his tracks but was soon out of breath and sweating beneath her layers of clothing. As the snow began to fall harder, she told herself this was a good thing. The storm would keep everyone at the camp inside and the snow would help muffle the sound of their approach.

After they'd walked for half an hour or so, Jack stopped. Andrea moved up beside him and looked down on the river some ten feet below. Ice rimmed the frothing brown water. "If we walk along the riverbank from here, we should come to the camp," he said.

She shivered, as much from fear of what lay ahead as from the cold soaking through her clothing. Jack pressed something into her hand—the key to his truck. "Do you think you can make it with Ian back to my truck by yourself?" he asked.

She stared up at him. "You're coming with us, aren't you?"

"I plan to. But just in case something happens—can you find your way by yourself?"

She folded her hand over the key, then slid it into her coat pocket. "I can do it. I follow the river, then turn left. That will eventually take me to the road. Your truck is parked just past the telephone pole with the sign tacked to it about a farm auction next month."

Jack clapped her shoulder. "Good job, remembering that sign."

"How's your leg?" she asked. All this hard hiking couldn't be good for his wounds.

"I'm fine. Don't worry about me." He turned away and started walking again before she could say anything else.

When he stopped again, she could make out the corner of a building maybe fifty yards ahead, the wood siding painted dark green, icicles hanging from the metal roof. Jack dropped to his knees and motioned for her to do likewise.

Snow soaked into her jeans and wet the cuffs of her coat as she crawled along behind Jack. She couldn't see anything from this height other than snow and Jack himself ahead of her. Then the undergrowth receded and they were in the clearing, behind a building. At the corner of the structure, Jack stood, his weapon drawn. She rose also, her back to the building, heart thudding painfully.

Jack peered around the side of the building. "What do you see?" she whispered.

"Nothing," he said. "But there are a lot of buildings here. We're going to have to get closer if we're going to find Ian."

The camp looked deserted, the windows in the cabins boarded up, the sign that read Office on one building hanging crooked from a single nail. But the tire tracks in the packed snow of the drive looked fresh, and the smell of wood smoke mingled with the scents of pine trees.

There were nine cabins overall, eight arranged in a half circle, with the office, a larger structure that looked as if it had once contained a residence as well as a store, sitting to one side, nearest the narrow drive that led from the main road. A rusting metal arch marked the entrance to the camp, the sign hanging from the top unreadable from Jack's position.

He waited, ears straining to hear any sound beyond the whistle of wind through the trees. The cabin they were standing behind was probably empty. In the five minutes or so they had been standing here, he hadn't heard any sounds from inside. If someone had so much as walked around in there, he and Andrea would have known about it.

Behind him, Andrea shifted her weight from foot to foot, feet crunching on the snow. He checked his watch. A few minutes past ten thirty. If Anderson or whoever he worked for was planning an ambush, they were probably already in place. They'd done a good job concealing themselves, though it would be easy enough to take up positions in the cabins and wait for Jack and Andrea to drive into the yard. Then the kidnappers could converge and take them prisoner or simply open fire and kill them before they had a chance to act.

Well, that wasn't going to happen. He was going to find Anderson and whoever else was here before they found him. But first he needed to know where they were keeping Ian.

He turned and leaned toward Andrea, his mouth against her ear. The vanilla-and-honey scent of her seemed out of place in the midst of danger, but it made him more determined than ever to save her son and get her out of harm's way as quickly as possible. "We're going to have to search the cabins," he whispered. "We'll approach from the back and listen for sounds of movement inside. If we don't hear anything from any of them, we'll have to try to get a look inside somehow, by prying the boards off the back window or something."

She nodded.

"I'll go first," he said. "When I give the signal, you run to me."

He checked the area again. Still no sign of life. He took a deep breath, blew it out, then made a dash for the next cabin in line.

Cursing his throbbing leg, he leaned against the

side of the building, waiting for his heart to slow and his breath to grow more even. No signs of movement in the yard. He looked toward Andrea and nodded. She didn't hesitate but raced toward him.

The back of the cabin contained a single boarded-up window. Jack pressed his ear to the plywood and Andrea did the same. She closed her eyes as she listened, so he took advantage of the moment to study her. Blueish half-moons beneath her eyes testified to her sleepless night, and tension traced fine lines around her mouth. Snow dusted the top of her head and the shoulders of her coat, and as he watched, a shiver ran through her. But she hadn't uttered a word of complaint.

She opened her eyes, and the sadness of her expression pulled at him. "I don't hear anything," she whispered.

He shook his head and indicated that they should move on to the next cabin.

Once again, they pressed their ears to the boarded-up back window and listened. Andrea's eyes widened as the low rumble of male voice reached them. Jack nodded and strained to make out the words. "Better…kid…boss…" Frowning, he drew back. Whoever was speaking was in the cabin's front room, too far away to be heard clearly. He pulled Andrea away from the building.

"I'm going around to the side," he said. "There's another window there. If I can hear their conversation, that might help us find Ian and figure out the best way to get to him."

"I'll go with you," she said.

"No. It's too dangerous. Anyone walking by the front of the cabin could see us."

"Two sets of ears are better than one," she said. "Besides, I think we'll both be safer if we stick together."

He didn't have time to waste arguing with her, and maybe she had a point. "All right. Let's go before they leave the cabin."

Two windows looked out from the side of the cabin. Jack led the way to the front window and crouched low beside it. Andrea moved in close behind him, bracing herself with one hand on his back. Her touch reminded him that there was more at stake with this mission than perhaps any other he had undertaken. He pressed his ear to the bottom of the plywood that covered the window.

"Where are they? Shouldn't they be here by now?" The speaker's voice was high and thin, with a flat Midwestern accent.

"It's not even eleven. They'll be here." The second speaker had a deeper, rougher voice, with no identifiable accent.

"This snow might slow them down. The radio said there's a winter storm warning."

"It's just a little snow. If they want to see their kid, they'll be here."

"We can't screw this up. Not after what happened last time." Footsteps followed these words, as if the first man had begun to pace.

"You and I don't have to worry about that. We'll blame the kid getting away on Leo."

Andrea lurched against him. Jack reached out a hand to steady her and squeezed her arm.

"That's not going to happen with this one," the first speaker said. "I told Leo not to let this one out of his sight."

"He's only what, five?" the second man said. "The other one was practically a grown man. We should have been more careful."

"It doesn't matter. His old man wasn't cooperating anyway. I say we tell the boss he was causing trouble and we finished him off. It's not like he's going to make us show him a body."

"I wouldn't put it past him. He doesn't overlook details like that."

"So we do a good job with the fed and he doesn't worry about anything else," the first man said.

"When they get here, I get first shot at the fed," the gravel-voiced man said. "In the gut, so that he dies slowly."

"Don't make a mess," the first man said. "We have to haul the body out of here. I don't want blood all over the car."

"I'm not worried about your car. If you had been thinking at all, you would have got a van. We wouldn't have to worry about anyone seeing inside one of those."

"There's no one out here to see into anything," the first man said. "What about the woman and the kid? What are we going to do with them?"

"What do you think?" Gravel Voice said.

"I ain't killing no little kid."

Andrea's fingers dug into Jack's back.

"I'll do it, then. Or Leo will do it. He already has orders to silence the kid if Prescott and the woman bring anybody else with them."

"As long as I don't have to do it," the first man said.

"We don't have a choice. He knows what we look like. We can't afford to leave him behind."

"The woman is pretty," the first man said. "We ought to keep her around for a little while."

"It's just like you to think that way. We haven't got time. The boss wants all of those feds out of the way."

"You mean Roland wants them out of the way," the first man said. "I'm not so sure the boss even knows what's going on. I think Roland is calling all the shots these days."

"You had better not let anyone else hear you say that—especially Roland."

"How much longer do we have to stay out here in the middle of nowhere? I'm ready to get back to the city."

"When the big job goes down, we'll be a part of that."

"Yeah, well, I've been hearing that for a while now and I ain't seen any sign that anything is going to happen. I think Roland and the rest of that bunch are just stringing us along."

"You're wrong," Gravel Voice said. "It would have happened before now if it wasn't for those feds. That's why what we're doing is so important. We get rid of them and the rest of the plan can be executed."

"Listen to you and your five-dollar words." The pacing stopped. "All right, let's go. I don't want Prescott and that woman sneaking into camp when we're not looking."

"They won't get past the traps we set," Gravel Voice said. "We'll know if they try to get in." Footsteps moved toward the door.

Jack grabbed Andrea's arm and they raced to the cover of the woods behind the cabin. The front door slammed and he caught a glimpse of two men moving away.

Neither of them said anything for a long moment as they caught their breath. Finally, Andrea leaned toward him. "What traps?" she asked.

Jack shook his head. "I don't know. Either he was bluffing, or we got lucky and didn't set off anything. I think the other man, the one with the higher voice, was Anderson, the man we saw in the restaurant."

"He mentioned seeing me before." A shudder ran

through her. Jack pushed down his own revulsion at the man and his proposal to keep Andrea alive for a while longer than the others. He couldn't deny that emotion added urgency to his desire to stop these men, but he couldn't let feelings guide him. He had to think coldly and logically and rely on his training.

"They were holding a child here before Ian," Andrea said. "And he got away."

"Not a little boy like Ian," Jack said. "They said this one was 'almost a grown man.' So a teenager." He frowned. "No one has reported a missing child in the area. Our office would have heard."

"Maybe the child wasn't from here," Andrea said.

"The names of missing children are in a national database. Still, we don't know when this happened."

"They talked as if they had been here awhile," she said. "Who is Roland?"

"Roland is part of the suspected terrorist cell we've been tracking." Roland had been Duane Braeswood's right-hand man, but it sounded as if, with Braeswood's injuries, he might be taking a more prominent role. Jack filed the information away to share with the team. "I can call in my team," he said. "They could be here in less than an hour and they've got the manpower and equipment to surround this place."

"No! You heard what they said—if anyone else shows up, they'll kill Ian."

"We'd have a plan to prevent that. I could move in right away to protect him."

"I won't take that kind of chance with my son." She gripped his arm, her fingers digging in. "I'm really afraid of these people," she said. "Not just for Ian's sake, but for yours. They hate you."

"Most of the people we hunt down hate us. That doesn't stop us."

"I knew the people Preston was trying to stop were terrible, and I thought I understood that they were dangerous. But I never met them or saw them, so the danger was always more abstract." She hugged herself. "This is so much more real and frightening."

"They're just people," he said. "They're not smarter or stronger or luckier than us. Don't underestimate them, but don't make them bigger than they are."

She took a deep breath and nodded. "You're right. That makes sense. What do we do now?"

"We need to figure out where they're hiding Ian, and we need to determine if anyone else is in the camp."

"They mentioned someone named Leo," she said. "It sounds as if he's with Ian."

"There may just be the three of them. If so, the odds aren't so bad. But we can't assume anything. We need to be sure."

The two men who had been speaking had moved in the direction of the office, so he and Andrea continued down the row of cabins, pausing to listen at each one. But all were silent and seemingly empty. After another twenty minutes or so, they reached the last cabin in line. Smaller than the others, it was also farthest from the entrance. The kidnappers might have chosen it as the best place to keep Ian for these reasons.

Jack paused by the back window and sniffed the damp air. "Do you smell that?" he asked.

"What?" Andrea tilted her head back and sniffed also.

"Wood smoke. It's stronger here. As if someone had a fire in the woodstove recently." He stepped back and looked up at the black stovepipe that jutted from the roof. No smoke curled from it, but the odor in the chill air told him it might have, and recently.

They pressed their ears to the plywood over the back window, tensed. Jack listened to the roaring of his own pulse. After a long moment Andrea's shoulders slumped and she shook her head. "I don't hear—"

Thump!

They both jumped and Andrea covered her mouth to stifle a cry. She stared at the window, then pressed her ear to the plywood once more. The sound came again. *Thump! Thump! Thump!*

"Hey! Knock it off, kid. Be still in there!" The man's voice was broad and nasal, definitely not either of the two men they had overheard earlier. It was a good bet they had found Leo.

Andrea practically vibrated with tension. She hugged Jack to her, then released him. *What do we do now?* she mouthed.

They could burst into the cabin and try to overpower whoever was in there with the boy—if Ian really was the one making those noises—but they risked being trapped if Anderson and Gravel Voice came running. And they still weren't certain there weren't other men in the camp. He pulled Andrea away from the cabin, back into the woods, where they could talk with less chance of being overheard.

"We need to find out for certain how many people we're up against," he said.

Her gaze darted back to the cabin. Her focus now was on her son. "How do we do that?"

He needed a way to draw them out without endangering Ian or Andrea. The scent of wood smoke tickled his nose, giving him an idea. "If we set one of the empty cabins on fire, that will draw them out," he said. "While they're distracted, we'll run in and grab Ian."

She frowned. "How are we going to set anything on fire when it's snowing?"

"We need an accelerant. Gasoline or kerosene or something like that."

"Where are we going to get that?"

"There might be some up by the office. It looks

like it used to be a store. We'll need matches or a lighter, too."

"Why can't we just go in, grab Ian and get out of here? We both have guns, and if we're fast, we'll be gone before whoever is in there guarding him can call for help."

"We still have to make it back to my truck without them catching us," he said. "We can't exactly move quickly in this rough country, in the snow, carrying a child. They might cut us off or corner us."

"What if they do that now, before we can get to Ian?"

"If we can't find what we need to start a fire, then we may very well have to grab him and make a run for it. But let's try it my way first."

She sighed. "All right."

"You stay here," he said. "I'll check the office. If I find what I need, I'll start the fire. As soon as Ian's guard leaves, you go in and get Ian. But be ready to shoot if you run into a second guard."

"What do I do if I see someone heading your way?" she asked.

If this were an FBI operation, they would have radio communication, but Andrea hadn't even had time to replace the cell phone Anderson had stolen. "Stay out of sight," he said. "Look after yourself and Ian. I'll watch out for myself."

He retraced his route behind the row of cabins. The snow was falling harder now, a white curtain over the landscape. The compound remained empty and silent save for the soft crunch of their footsteps. He would be able to hear a car approaching in the storm, if reinforcements showed up in anticipation of Jack and Andrea's scheduled arrival with the ransom money.

Like the other buildings in the camp, the office was a simple rectangular board-and-batten structure with a small front porch, a metal roof and boarded-up windows. But this building was twice as large as the others and boasted a back entrance in addition to the front door. Jack hoped this back door led to a storeroom where he could find the materials he needed for starting a fire.

The steps leading to the back door had long since rotted away, but someone had positioned a plastic milk crate on the ground below the threshold, which enabled Jack to reach the doorknob. The door was locked, but the mechanism was cheap and flimsy. He took out his pocketknife and had the lock open in less than a minute.

As soon as the door was open, Jack slipped inside and closed it again. The interior of the building was black and smelled of mouse and mold. He waited, his back to the door, and allowed his eyes to adjust to the dimness. After a few minutes he could make out the bulky shapes of stacked boxes and old furniture. A second, closed door must lead into the main part of the building. He pressed his ear to it and listened. Nothing.

Confident that he was alone, Jack risked switching on the flashlight on his phone. He played the beam across the piled junk in the storeroom: a sagging upholstered armchair, a leaning stack of yellowing newspapers, a table with a broken leg, some old flowerpots, a case of bottled water and another of chicken noodle soup, several unlabeled cardboard boxes, and a shelving unit filled with canned goods—some of them so old the labels were barely legible.

No gas cans. No cans of kerosene. Treading carefully, Jack moved over to the canned-goods shelf. He scanned the items there—mostly beans and canned peaches or tomatoes. But on the bottom shelf he found a gallon container of cooking oil. If he let the oil soak into the dry wood of one of the cabins, he might be able to get a good blaze going in spite of the damp.

He picked up the oil and flinched when a mouse raced out from behind it. Heart pounding, he searched the shelves for matches or a lighter. Behind a box of assorted fishing flies he found a butane lighter, the long-handled kind used to light campfires or candles. Perfect.

He pocketed the lighter, switched off the flashlight and stowed the phone, then picked up the cooking oil. He stopped beside the pile of newspapers and stuffed a few under his jacket to use as kindling. Andrea was probably wondering what had happened to him. He hoped she was staying put and not attempting anything rash. She struck him as a controlled, reasonable woman, but a mother whose child was in danger had plenty of reasons to set aside caution.

Outside once more, the cold wind hit him with a force that made him grit his teeth and hunch against the onslaught. His leg throbbed from the dampness and his recent exertions. A hot blaze was going to feel good, though he wouldn't have time to enjoy it.

He stopped at the corner of the office and thus the most distant point from the building where Ian was being held. Or at least, they had assumed the thumping noise came from Ian. Assumptions were dangerous in his business, but what other "kid" would Anderson and his men be keeping prisoner out here?

What about the boy or teenager or whoever he was they had alluded to earlier? The two men they overheard said he had escaped, but where had he gone? And why hadn't the FBI heard anything about this?

He dropped the container of cooking oil at the back corner of the building and wadded the papers against the foundation, sheltering them from the snowfall as best he could with his body. When he was satisfied with the arrangement, he uncapped the bottle of oil and splashed it onto the side of the building. The siding, even damp from the storm, sucked up the oil, which smelled rancid, as if it had sat in that storeroom for many years. Careful not to get any oil on himself, Jack emptied the bottle, tossed it aside, then pulled out the lighter.

"Don't make another move, Agent Prescott, or I'll blow a hole through your guts."

Chapter Five

Andrea's stomach churned with nerves as she waited for something to happen. Would Jack really be able to set a fire in all this snow? Would he even find anything to start a blaze with? And if he did, would she be able to get inside the cabin and rescue Ian before someone spotted her?

She drew the gun from the back of her jeans and eased off the safety. Then she pressed her ear to the plywood covering the window and listened. Someone was moving around in there—someone a lot bigger than Ian, from the sound of it. What had they done to her poor baby? Was he tied up? Gagged?

She took a deep breath. No time to panic here. She could be furious about all this later. Right now she had to be calm. Cold as ice. She was a woman on a mission to save her son and she couldn't afford to think about anything else.

What was taking Jack so long? She had expected flames by now. Shouting. Slamming doors. People running to put out the fire. At the very least, she expected Jack to come back and tell her they were going to have to go to plan B, whatever that was.

Still holding the gun with both hands, stiff-armed and pointed at the ground the way she'd seen on TV, she crept to the other end of the building. She had to move out a few steps in order to see the first cabin in line. Something shifted in the curtain of snow. Then Jack stepped out of the shadows beside the building.

And another man, dressed in the kind of camouflage coveralls hunters sometimes wore, a stocking cap pulled low over his forehead, stepped out behind Jack. Andrea gasped and started toward them, then thought better of it. The last thing she wanted was for Jack's captor to spot her. She shrank back against the building. *Think!* she ordered her brain, which had frozen in fear, like a streamed movie stuck buffering.

There was still someone moving around in the cabin with Ian. So the man with Jack was probably one of the two men they had overheard earlier—or maybe he was a fourth man. There might be any number of people hidden in the other cabins or in the woods nearby. Her stomach churned at the idea and she forced it from her mind. Right now she needed to get closer to Jack and his captor and try to figure things out. At least that way she could find out where they were taking Jack.

Keeping close to the cabins and moving as quickly and quietly as possible, she crept toward the office building. She stopped at the corner of the last cabin before the office and her stomach plummeted as Jack's captor prodded him up onto the office's front porch and in through the door. Raised voices sounded from the office—at least two men in addition to Jack, who, as far as she could determine, wasn't talking.

Two men in the office, plus one person in the cabin with Ian—three people besides her and Jack in the camp. Were there more in the other cabins? They hadn't bothered to show themselves. Maybe while the two in the office were dealing with Jack, she should bust into the end cabin, shoot the guy with Ian and rescue her son.

And leave Jack to die? Nausea rose in her throat at the thought. She flipped the safety back on the gun, stuffed it in the waistband of her jeans and pushed a wet lock of hair out of her eyes. At least all this cold was shocking her out of the stupor she'd slipped into the moment she had discovered her son was missing. Why hadn't she called the police or let Jack call his colleagues with the Bureau?

That was easy enough to answer—she hadn't wanted to do anything to jeopardize Ian's safety. The kidnappers had counted on that. It was the same psychology that made people fall for scammers who posed as stranded grandchildren who needed money to get out of jail. The grandparents who fell prey to such traps were so worried about the safety of their loved ones that they didn't think logically. She would have judged herself too savvy and educated to fall for such a ruse, but at least when it came to children, apparently, emotion trumped common sense every time.

Though there were no windows on this side of the office building, she still worried someone might spot her, so she moved along the side of the cabin to the back. She stopped and studied the structure again. It was built like all the others, except that this one was larger and also included a back door. How could she help Jack? Alone, she wasn't sure she had the nerve to burst in there, waving the pistol around as if she knew what she was doing. That would probably distract his captors for a few seconds—until they shot her or overpowered her.

Her gaze shifted to the back door. Maybe she could creep in that way and get the jump on them. There weren't any steps leading up to the door, but someone—Jack?—had positioned a milk crate underneath it. She frowned at the other items near the crate—an overturned plastic jug and what looked like a bunch of paper.

She glanced toward the front of the building—no movement. Then she raced toward the back door. The empty gallon jug lay on its side in the mud, a camping lighter beside it. The label on the jug read Cooking Oil. The paper—yellowing newsprint—was crumpled around the corner of the cabin. The outer layer of paper was soaked, but when she pulled this away, she found a drier layer. Maybe dry enough to light.

Muffled voices rumbled from the office at the front of the building, but she couldn't make out any words. If she set the fire as Jack had planned, she could force Jack's captors out of there. But would Jack be in even more danger, trapped in flames?

It would take a while for the building to burn down, so she didn't think Jack was in much danger. And getting his captors away from him and occupied with putting out the blaze would give them all more time to escape. "Here goes nothing," she muttered, and flicked the lighter. The paper flared instantly, and seconds later, flames licked at the old wood of the cabin. Andrea retreated to the edge of the woods and waited.

ANDERSON SHOVED THE rifle barrel into the small of Jack's back and Jack took another step forward into the front room of the office. He studied the man who lounged on a faded green sofa, keeping his expression impassive. This man was older than Anderson, maybe midfifties, with a hawk nose and deeply recessed eyes. Nothing about him was familiar. He wasn't in the database Jack had combed through last night and he wasn't on the hours of surveillance videos from terrorist targets the team had reviewed.

"We were beginning to think you had stood us up, Agent Prescott," the man said, his voice gravelly and low—the other man Jack and Andrea had overheard earlier. "Of course, I expected you to do something underhanded, which is why my friend here was watching for you."

Jack remained silent, giving nothing away.

"Did you bring the money we asked for?" the man asked.

"Does your boss know you only asked for ten thousand?" Jack asked. "That seems pretty small-time for a guy like him. That kind of money won't pay his expenses for a day."

The man's eyes shifted, uncertain. "I'm the only boss around here," he said, though to Jack's ears the words carried more bluster than conviction.

"So Braeswood and Roland don't have anything to do with this," Jack said. "You just happened to know my name and what I do and who I'm connected to. And you came up with the idea to kidnap that little boy to get to me all by yourself."

"Are you saying you don't think I'm smart enough to come up with an idea like that?" He stood.

"If you were smarter, you wouldn't be stuck out here in the middle of nowhere, babysitting a kid," Jack said. "Braeswood would have given you something more important to do."

A vein pulsed at the corner of Gravel Voice's right eye. "This isn't about the kid," he said. "It's about you and the rest of the jackbooted thugs who pass yourselves off as law enforcement in this country."

"Jackbooted thugs. I haven't heard that one in a while. Classic conspiracy-theorist rhetoric. Did they teach you that in the indoctrination camps?" If he made the man mad enough, would he blurt out something Jack could use later to tie him to Braeswood's group? Gravel Voice hadn't denied the connection, a sign that Jack's assumption of a connection was on the money.

Anderson, who had remained still and silent all this time, suddenly spoke. "Do you smell something funny?"

Gravel Voice glared at him. "What do you mean?" He sniffed. "All I smell is wood smoke."

The tang of wood smoke hung in the air, stronger than it had been earlier, Jack thought.

"Didn't you tell Leo to put out that fire?" Gravel Voice asked.

"He put it out. I watched him do it," Anderson said.

"He must have lit it again," Gravel Voice said. "I smell smoke."

Anderson made a face. "He was whining about being cold. He don't like being stuck down there with the kid."

"It's not like he's got the tough job, guarding a toddler. He's just a whiner. Go tell him to put the fire out. Somebody is going to smell it and come nosing around."

Anderson glanced at Jack. "What about him?"

Gravel Voice pulled out a pistol—a long-barreled .44. The kind of gun that would blow a hole the size of a dinner plate in Jack at this close range. "He'll be fine here with me."

"Okay." Anderson slouched out the door, leaving Jack and his boss alone.

"Where's the woman?" Gravel Voice asked. Then, as if there might be more than one woman involved, he clarified, "The boy's mom."

"I came alone," Jack said.

"Liar." The gunshot echoed off the walls, leaving Jack's ears ringing. The bullet bit into the door-frame behind Jack's head. "Where is she?" Gravel Voice shouted.

"I don't know," Jack said. True enough. He hoped Andrea had stayed behind the last cabin, but he had no way of knowing.

The front door burst open, hitting against the wall. "Fire!" Anderson yelled.

The smell of smoke was much stronger now. "What the—?" Gravel Voice leaped to his feet.

"This building is on fire!" Anderson shouted. "You need to get out now, Jerry." Not waiting for an answer, he ran outside again.

Gravel Voice looked toward the door, then at Jack. "I don't have time to waste with you," he said, and raised the pistol.

The gunshot exploded through the room. Gravel Voice staggered forward, a stunned expression on his

face, then sank to his knees, blood staining the front
of his shirt, his own weapon unfired. Jack lunged and
twisted the gun from his hand, then looked past him
as Andrea stepped through the door from the storeroom, the Beretta in her hand.

"Let's go," Jack said. Still holding the .44, he
grabbed her free hand and pulled her toward the
back door.

"Is he dead?" she asked, looking over her shoulder toward the man's slumped figure.

"I don't know." Probably. He doubted anyone
could survive a direct hit like that.

"He was going to kill you," she said,

"Yes. You saved my life." He pulled her along
after him. They could talk through her guilt or confusion or whatever she was feeling later. Right now
they had to take advantage of the opportunity they
had. "Come on," he said. "We have to hurry."

"Where are we going?" she asked as they ran out
the front door, across the porch and around the side
of the building, which was completely engulfed in
flames now. In spite of the damp, the old, dry wood
had caught quickly.

Jack put up a hand to shield his face from the intense heat and guided her around the back of the row
of cabins. "We're going to get Ian!" he shouted over
the crackle of the flames.

As they raced past the opening between the first
and second cabins, he caught a glimpse of the com-

motion in the front of the buildings. Anderson raced past, shouting, but not at Jack and Andrea. Right now all his attention was on the burning building, but before too long, someone would remember the outsiders and come looking for them. They had to act quickly.

Jack and Andrea reached the last cabin in time to see a compact, balding man emerge from the building. He stared toward the flames, then took off running.

Jack didn't hesitate, but raced into the cabin. Inside, Andrea pushed past him. "Ian!" she called. "Ian, Mommy's here!"

Frantic thumping led them to a back room, where Ian lay on a mattress on the floor. Though his hands and feet were tied and a bandanna served as a gag, he kicked his feet against the floor. "Oh, Ian!" Andrea knelt and pulled her son close.

Jack joined her and worked the knot on the bandanna loose and removed the gag. "We'll untie you later, buddy," he said, scooping the boy out of Andrea's arms and standing, biting down hard to keep from crying out as pain shot through his injured leg. "Right now we have to get out of here."

After checking to make sure no one was looking their way, he ran out of the cabin and around the side, into the woods behind the camp. They made no attempt at stealth this time as they slogged through the heavy snow, followed the riverbank back toward where he had parked his truck. Behind him, he heard

Andrea stumbling through drifts and shoving aside the branches of scrub oak and piñon.

Ian lay still in Jack's arms, staring up at him with huge, frightened eyes. "It's okay, buddy," Jack said. "You're safe now."

"Jack!" Andrea's scream froze him. He whirled to find her tangled in camouflage netting. She clawed at the wet jute that covered her head and shoulders.

"Hang on—let me help." He carefully laid Ian on the ground. "Hang on just a minute, buddy," he told the boy. "I'm going to get your mom."

He approached her slowly, wary of any other traps. The netting had dropped from a tree overhead and Andrea was thoroughly tangled, her legs and arms partially protruding from the mesh, her body tilted upside down. "Hold still and I'll cut you loose," he said. He pulled out his pocketknife and began sawing at the thick jute.

"Hurry," she pleaded. "They could be right behind us."

"Just a few more cuts… There!" He sliced at a last cord and pulled the netting from around her. "This must be one of the traps they set for us," he said. "We were lucky we didn't run into one on our way to the camp."

"Let's hope our luck holds out." She looked over her shoulder. "Do you think they realize we're gone yet?"

The noise from the camp faded, and it had begun

to snow harder. The fire might already be out. Anderson and Leo had probably checked the cabin by now and discovered that Ian had disappeared. "We'd better hurry," he said, and picked up Ian again.

Another five minutes of stumbling through the woods and he spotted the truck up ahead. "Do you have the keys?" he called over his shoulder.

Andrea moved alongside him and hit the button to unlock the vehicle. She ran ahead and opened the passenger door. He deposited Ian inside, then took his knife from his pocket and handed it to her. "You can cut him loose while I drive," he said, taking the key from her and moving around to the driver's side.

"Oh, honey, I'm so glad to see you," she said as she slid into the passenger seat and pulled Ian onto her lap. Jack was sure those were tears running down her cheeks and not melted snow, though the storm had returned in earnest, a blanket of white falling from the sky.

"Anderson and Leo are probably looking for us by now," he said as the truck's engine roared to life.

"Do you think there were others?" she asked, her arms tight around Ian.

"I didn't see any sign of anyone else. I think it was just the three of them." Two now, he thought. "They'll have a hard time catching up to us now." At least, he hoped that was the case. He had no idea what kind of arsenal those three had at their disposal. Previous experience with Braeswood's group had suggested they had almost limitless resources. Braeswood had a fortune of his own and had managed to recruit more than a few wealthy donors to his cause. Plus, the Bureau suspected foreign groups contributed to his efforts. The feds, on the other hand, had to deal with numerous budget constraints.

"Those are bad men," Ian said.

"They are," Andrea agreed. "But you were very brave." She sawed at the ropes that bound his hands. Once they were severed, she turned her attention to the ties around his ankles.

"I peed my pants." Ian sounded as if he was about to cry as he made this confession. "I couldn't help it. The man wouldn't untie me so I could go to the bathroom."

"It's okay, honey," Andrea said. "That doesn't matter. And the snow has washed you all off now anyway."

"There are some blankets behind the seat you can wrap up in," Jack said. He hit the controls to turn up the heat. Now that they were out of the storm, a chill was setting in. He had to gun the engine to guide the truck through the fast-accumulating snow. He braked at the edge of the woods and prepared to turn out onto the road. As soon as they were well away from the camp, he would call his team and let them know to be on the lookout for Anderson and the rest.

He nosed the truck up onto the shoulder of the road, then stopped to wait for a car to pass. "Do you think the people in that car could see the fire at the camp from the road?" Andrea asked.

"They saw the fire, all right," Jack said, his fingers tightening around the steering wheel. "That was Anderson driving, and Ian's guard, Leo, was beside him."

"Where are they going?" Ian asked, his face creased with worry.

"They're running away, honey." Andrea pulled Ian against her, as if to hide him from his kidnappers.

Or they were looking for their escaped prisoner. Or rushing Gravel Voice to the hospital. But Jack didn't want to say anything to upset Ian more. Better the boy see them as having the upper hand. Which, in this case, maybe they did have. He shifted into gear and roared out onto the highway, the back end of the truck fishtailing as he fought for purchase on the slick pavement. He glanced toward Andrea and Ian. "Buckle up," he said. "We're going after them."

ANDREA WRAPPED BOTH arms around Ian and braced her feet against the floorboards as the truck rocketed down the snow-covered pavement in pursuit of Ian's captors. She couldn't believe that after all they had risked to get away from these guys, Jack was going after them. "Leave them," she pleaded. "Let the police take care of this. I just need to get Ian home."

"If we let them go, they're liable to come after

you again." Jack hunched over the steering wheel, his expression grim.

The thought sent an icy cold through her that the truck's roaring heater couldn't touch.

"Mom, you're squeezing me too tight." Ian squirmed and shoved against her.

"Sorry, honey." She loosened her hold and he shifted around to sit in her lap, facing forward. She tried not to think what would happen if they crashed. But she hadn't thought to bring Ian's booster seat with her, and now didn't seem the right time to try to belt him into the backseat. "Don't be scared," she said. "Everything is going to be all right."

"I'm not scared," he said. Eyes bright, he focused on the taillights of the car ahead of him. "This is just like in the movies."

What kind of movies has he been watching? she wondered as the truck skidded around a curve. They were close enough to read the Colorado license plate on the car ahead, but the kidnappers hadn't slowed down. "I just hope they don't start shooting at us," she said.

"Get down!" Jack shouted as the muzzle of a gun appeared in the passenger window.

She dived to the floorboards, on top of Ian. "Mom!" he yelped.

"Just stay still, honey." She closed her eyes, waiting for the shots she was sure were coming.

Instead, she heard the whine of the tires change

cadence. "We're crossing the first bridge," Jack said. "The road's getting icy, but I think we can make it."

Think? But the tires found purchase and she breathed a sigh of relief. She raised her head, trying to see what was going on.

"Stay down," Jack said. "They might try to fire at us again."

"What are they doing?" she asked.

"They've sped up." He pressed down on the accelerator and the truck fishtailed, sliding back and forth as he fought to bring it under control. Jack shook his head. "The road's too slick. They're having a hard time, too."

"They'll have to slow down at the second bridge, won't they?" she asked. She remembered a rickety-looking wooden structure, scarcely two lanes wide.

"They ought to, but with the snow coming down, they may be worried about getting to the highway before it becomes impossible to travel."

"What happens if we can't reach the highway?" she asked.

"We'll be stuck on this side until the weather clears."

And the bad guys might be stuck with them. Her stomach clenched at the idea and she hugged Ian more tightly.

"Why are we down here on the floor?" he whined. "I want to sit up where I can see."

"That isn't safe, honey. We can't get up until Jack tells us to."

"This is a dumb game," Ian said.

Andrea only wished it were a game. "Just stay down there until I tell you the coast is clear," Jack said. "Do that, and you'll win a special prize."

"What prize?" Ian asked.

"Do you like race cars?" Jack asked.

"Yes!"

"I have a friend who owns a real race car. I'll get him to take us for a ride in it."

"Wow!" Ian pressed himself even closer to the floorboard of the truck. Clearly, nothing Andrea could have offered would have appealed to him more than the prospect of a daredevil ride in a real race car. Never mind that they were already racing much too fast down a snow-slicked road. Apparently, in their brief acquaintance Jack had already figured out something about her son that she hadn't known— that Ian had a love for speed. She was both touched that he had paid so much attention to the boy and disturbed that there was something about her son she hadn't known. Was this only the first of many secrets that would be hidden from her because she was female?

"We're almost to the second bridge," Jack said. The truck slowed, then stopped altogether.

"What is it?" Andrea asked. "What's wrong?"

"The road is blocked. It looks like an avalanche from the cliffs above."

"What is Anderson doing?"

"He's stopped, too… Now he's backing up."

Andrea sat up. "Is he trying to ram us?"

Jack put the truck into Reverse. "I don't know." He began backing up as well, putting more distance between them and the sedan.

But Anderson didn't ram them. Instead, he stopped again, about a hundred yards back from the bridge. Then his brake lights went out and tires screeched as he shot forward. "What is he doing?" Andrea asked.

"I think he's going to try to bust through the snow," Jack said.

"Can they do that?" she asked.

"So far, they've proved they won't let anything keep them from getting what they want," he said, his expression grim. "But I won't let them succeed this time."

Chapter Six

Wanting to close her eyes but unable to look away, Andrea sat up and stared in horror as the sedan hit the wall of ice and snow. A spray of white exploded up on either side as the car hit the obstacle, then skewed sideways. The driver fought for control, but the car slid off the pavement and into a deep drift. "They're not going to make it," she said.

Smoke poured from beneath the battered hood. "They're not going anywhere now," Jack said. He started the truck and rolled forward.

"What are you doing?" she asked.

"I want to be close enough to nab them when they bail and make a run for it."

The sedan's driver shoved open his door, but he managed to force it only a couple of inches before the snow blocked it. A few seconds later, Anderson climbed from the driver's side window. Leo exited from the other side. Jack stepped out of the truck and drew his gun.

"This way, gentlemen," he shouted. "Keep your hands where I can see them and no one gets hurt."

Anderson glared at Jack. He shouted a curse, then climbed onto the bridge railing and dived into the rushing water. On the other side of the bridge, Leo jumped, as well.

Cursing under his breath, Jack began peeling off his jacket. "What are you doing?" Andrea asked..

"I'm going to pull them out before they drown." He bent to untie his boots. "And then I'm going to arrest them."

"Jack, that water is freezing. And the current is really fast. They're not worth it."

But he kept peeling off his coat. Snow plastered his shirt to his back, his muscles rippling as they moved. When he turned to face her, she stared at a single melted snowflake making its way down his throat.

"Andrea."

She swallowed hard and told herself to breathe again. Now was definitely not the time to be lusting after a man. He'd just…surprised her. She'd been so focused all day on saving Ian that she had forgotten how strong and good-looking Jack was. He pressed the .44 he had taken from one of the kidnappers into her hands. "Keep this for me." Then he handed her his shoulder holster with the Glock. "And this."

"You can't go after them unarmed."

"The guns are no use to me soaked in the river,

either." He touched her cheek and gave her a half smile. "Don't worry. I'm a strong swimmer."

He was also recovering from a gunshot wound. No matter how much he pretended otherwise, she knew the wound still bothered him. As he made his way toward the bridge, clad in only jeans and a flannel shirt, she detected the slight hesitation every time he put weight on his injured leg.

"Where is Jack going?" Ian asked. While she and Jack had argued, the boy had climbed onto the seat beside her.

She sighed. "He's going to do his job," she said. A job he clearly took very seriously. Just like Preston. The night her husband had died had been like this. She had begged him not to go on that raid. He was officially off duty and the SWAT team was prepared to handle things.

"It's my case," he had said as he'd slipped on his Kevlar vest, then buttoned up his shirt. "I need to be there."

She'd stood at the front door, baby Ian in her arms, and watched him walk away from her, toward danger. *He is always going to choose duty over his family*, she had thought to herself. It was the way things were supposed to be, but that didn't make it any easier for her to live with.

She slid out of the truck. "You stay inside," she told Ian. "You can watch out the window."

With the shoulder holster draped around her and

the .44 in her left hand, she took a few steps toward the bridge until she had a clear view of Jack making his way down the snowy embankment and of Anderson in the icy water. She couldn't see the other man, on the other side of the bridge, but Anderson was making slow but steady progress toward the opposite shore. Waves swamped him, and he had been carried a ways downstream, but before Jack reached the water's edge, Anderson crawled out onto the bank.

The kidnapper looked at Jack, then turned to look downstream. The other man stumbled toward him. Jack stood with his hands on his hips, staring after him. Leo made a rude gesture in his direction, and then both men began walking up the road, soon disappearing from view in the curtain of snow.

Andrea walked out to meet Jack. "I'm sorry they got away," she said. "But I'm not sorry you didn't have to go in after them."

"I couldn't be any colder than I am already." He followed her back toward the truck. "How's Ian?"

"He's okay. He's a lot calmer about all of this than I am."

"Kids are a lot tougher than we think sometimes. And he's with you now, so that makes everything all right."

"Everything doesn't feel all right. What are we going to do?"

He walked her around to the passenger side of the truck and held the door for her, then reached into the backseat and pulled out a gym bag. He grabbed a towel from it and rubbed at his hair as he walked around to the driver's side. "Hi, Jack," Ian said when Jack climbed into the truck. "You're wet."

"You're right, buddy. And I didn't even get to go swimming."

"It's snowing so hard you could almost go swimming on land," Ian said.

Jack laughed, and the boy joined in. The deep, masculine chuckles mingling with little-boy giggles made Andrea's breath catch. How was it possible to feel such joy and such fear at the same time? "You must be freezing," she said.

"I'll be okay." He shrugged back into his coat. "I've got a spare change of clothes here in the truck." He tossed the damp towel into the backseat, started the truck again and put it in gear. "We're going back to the camp," he said. "We can stay out of the weather in one of the cabins, get warm and decide what to do next."

JACK PARKED THE truck on the road and walked into the camp alone. This time, Andrea hadn't argued with him. She had slumped in the seat, her arms locked around her son, looking too exhausted for words. Ian, however, had cheerfully offered to come with him. "You'd better stay here, buddy," Jack had said, smiling in spite of his own weariness and the stabbing pain in his leg. "You'll get too cold out there."

"I like to play in the snow," he said.

Jack laughed. "Maybe we'll do that some other time. Right now I need you to stay with your mom and keep her company. She'd be pretty lonely if we both left her."

"Will you be back soon?" Ian asked.

"Soon. I promise."

He crept through the woods alongside the track leading into the camp and approached the compound obliquely, keeping an eye on both the entrance and the row of cabins. The office had been reduced to charred ruins, the acrid smell of smoke hovering in the air around it. The other buildings stood silent and still, their boarded-up fronts adding to their look of desolation.

He had reclaimed his Glock from Andrea and as he entered the camp, he drew it. Alert for any sign of life, he checked each cabin and found them all empty. The middle one, where they had overheard Anderson talking with Gravel Voice, contained a pair of faded green plaid recliners, a kitchen table and chairs, and a single mattress on an iron frame. The stale odors of cigarettes and coffee hung in the air. Jack was careful not to touch anything. An evidence team might be able to lift fingerprints or DNA from the furniture and kitchen utensils.

The end building, where Ian had been held, contained a sofa and a small table and a woodstove, as well as the mattress. The other cabins looked as if they hadn't been occupied by anything but mice and squirrels for years.

Jack left the camp and returned to the truck, grateful for the respite from the icy wind. "They're all gone," he said. "We'll be safe there. As soon as we're inside, I'll call my boss and fill him in."

"Do you think we'll have to stay here very long?" Andrea asked.

"I don't know. I'll get a weather report, too, and find out what the status is for the roads."

He parked the truck in front of the end cabin. Later he'd move the vehicle out of sight back in the trees, just in case anyone showed up again. "This one is in the best shape," he said. "And it has the woodstove, so wc can kcep warm."

"Warm sounds good." She picked up Ian and followed Jack up the steps. Ian made a noise of protest. "I don't like it here," he said.

"It's okay." Andrea rubbed his back and kissed the top of his head. "The bad men are gone and Jack and I are staying right here with you."

"I'm going to start a fire to warm us up." Jack knelt in front of the woodstove, relieved to see a supply of firewood against the back wall and a basket of kindling near the hearth. "We'll get dry. Then I'll see what I can find for dinner."

The boy didn't say anything, but he seemed content to sit in Andrea's lap on the sofa and watch Jack build the fire. Soon he had a good blaze going. He closed the glass-fronted door to the little stove. "That should warm us up quickly," he said. He stood. "I'm going to get my things out of the truck. You might look around here and see what kind of supplies we have."

He retrieved his gym bag from behind the seat and brought it inside, along with the damp towel. When he returned, he found Ian wrapped in a blanket and Andrea draping the boy's wet clothing on chairs in front of the fire. She looked up when he entered. "There's a lot of canned food and some dishes in the kitchen cabinets," she said. "And I found sheets and blankets for the bed."

"You should get out of those damp clothes," he said. "You'll feel a lot better when you're dry."

"Maybe." She looked doubtful.

"You can wrap up in a blanket," he said. "I promise not to look." But he wouldn't promise not to let his imagination fill in the details about her figure. The damp had made her clothing formfitting, making it pretty obvious that she was a very shapely woman. Even exhausted from their ordeal, her hair a wet tangle about her shoulders and any makeup she might have once worn long since washed away, she made him want to do things that might have made her blush if they had been alone and he had revealed his desires.

He turned away. They weren't alone, and they

weren't out of danger yet. He picked up his bag. "I'll change in the other room," he said.

After he had finished dressing in the sweats and a sleeveless T-shirt he usually wore to the gym, Jack called his boss. "Sir, this is Jack Prescott."

"Agent Prescott." Special Agent in Charge Ted Blessing had a deep, sonorous voice and the demeanor of a drill sergeant, which Jack suspected he had once been.

"Sir, I'm involved in a situation I believe relates to our case."

"Agent Prescott, you are on a medical leave. You are supposed to go to doctor's appointments and go home. How did you become involved in a 'situation'?"

"I was at a medical appointment, sir. Or at least, I went to see a therapist I hoped could help me remember who killed Gus Mathers." He had to force out the words. Admitting he had sought help from a counselor felt like confessing to a weakness.

"And what happened?" Blessing asked.

Jack explained about spotting Anderson in the restaurant, the theft of Andrea's purse and the subsequent kidnapping of her son.

"Why didn't you call me and alert the local police as soon as Dr. McNeil contacted you?" Blessing's words held an edge sharp enough to cut.

"She insisted I keep quiet," Jack said. "The note

left at her house said if she contacted anyone other than me, the kidnappers would kill her son."

"The note specifically mentioned you."

"It said she could call her boyfriend, but she doesn't have a boyfriend. Anderson saw us together in the restaurant. I think he assumed a relationship." From the first he had felt drawn to Andrea, but he couldn't possibly have given that away over a casual lunch, could he?

"We're going to set aside the question of why you were having lunch with your therapist—for now," Blessing said. "What happened next?"

"The next morning a man called and instructed us to bring the ransom money to an address, which turned out to be an abandoned fishing camp on the Pine River, near the small town of Bayfield. We arrived early and hiked in to assess the situation. We located the boy and determined there were three men in the camp—Anderson and two others I had never seen before."

"And you still didn't call the police?"

"We were concerned if authorities arrived, the kidnappers would carry out their threat to murder the boy. Then the kidnappers discovered our presence. After an exchange of gunfire, one of them was killed. The other two fled."

Blessing made a sound like grinding his teeth. "I'll expect a full report detailing why you discharged your weapon—in triplicate."

"Yes, sir." Jack would fill in the details later to clarify that it was Andrea who had fired, killing a man in order to save Jack's life. "I pursued the remaining two kidnappers as far as the river. An avalanche had blocked the road and they ran their car into a ditch. They fled on foot and jumped into the river and swam the rest of the way across and escaped. If you can get some men out here, you might be able to pick them up."

"Where are you and Dr. McNeil now?" Blessing asked.

"We're back at the fishing camp with her son. We're stuck here until the weather clears."

"Are you all right?"

"Yes, sir. No one is hurt and we have food and shelter."

"The weather report is calling for blizzard conditions to continue into the night, so plan to stay put," Blessing said. "Give me some directions and a description of the two men we're looking for and I'll get some agents out there. I'll also alert local authorities."

Jack gave directions and descriptions. "What makes you think this is connected to our case?" Blessing asked. "Is it because of Anderson?"

"Yes, sir. He's in our database of suspected associates of the terrorist cell we've been tracking. Also, Dr. McNeil and I overheard Anderson talking with the man who was shot, and they mentioned Roland.

There was also another man, their boss, whom they didn't mention by name, but I think they were talking about Braeswood. They implied that this bigger boss wasn't in a position to keep tabs on the operation right now, and Roland had taken over. That fits the scenario of Braeswood recovering from wounds sustained when he jumped off that railroad bridge."

"Having another man named Roland involved would be a big coincidence," Blessing said. "But we both know coincidences do happen in our line of work. The information you've given me is very interesting, but we'll have to dig deeper to find proof of a connection. It's possible, even more reasonable, to believe the kidnappers targeted Dr. McNeil for a specific reason. Has she suggested anything in her past or her other relationships that might lead her to be targeted?"

"Her late husband was a police officer who died in the line of duty three years ago," Jack said. "But she's sure this doesn't have anything to do with him. And this whole scenario echoes methods the group has used before. I think Anderson kidnapped Ian McNeil in order to get to me."

"It sounds as if it almost worked. I'll look into it. In the meantime, sit tight until the weather clears."

Jack ended the call and returned to the front room. Andrea still stood in front of the fire, shivering in her wet clothes in spite of the blaze. He pressed a sweatshirt and socks into her hands. "Put these on," he said. "You'll feel better."

"All right." She glanced toward Ian, but the boy was curled on his side on the sofa, sound asleep.

While Andrea changed, Jack hung his jeans and shirt to dry, then went into the kitchen, where he found coffee and a coffeepot. He got the coffee started on the little three-burner gas stove, then opened two cans of chili, dumped them into a saucepan and started that heating. A few minutes later, Andrea, wearing his sweatshirt, which came to midthigh, and a pair of his gym socks, shuffled into the kitchen. He let his gaze linger briefly on her long, shapely legs before he forced himself to turn away.

"What smells so good?" she asked. "I'm starved."

"Canned chili. We'll have it with crackers. Do you think Ian will wake up and eat some?"

"I hate to wake him, but if the men holding him wouldn't even let him go to the bathroom, I doubt they fed him anything to eat." Her face crumpled and he thought she might cry.

He pulled her close and held her tightly against him. "It's okay," he murmured. "He's safe now, and they didn't hurt him."

"Thanks to you." She lifted her head to look into his eyes. "I don't know what I would have done without you," she said. "I never could have rescued him on my own. I owe you everything."

"You don't owe me anything," he said. "You saved my life, remember?"

He was sorry as soon as he said the words. She stiffened and bowed her head and he silently cursed his thoughtlessness. He should never have reminded her of the man she had shot, who had probably died and whose burned body he suspected lay somewhere in the wreckage of the office. "Andrea, look at me," he said.

She raised her eyes to meet his. "You did the right thing," he said. "If you hadn't fired when you did, he would have killed me. And then he would have killed you, and probably Ian, too."

She took a deep breath and her shoulders straightened. "You're right, of course. I just... I never expected to have to do something like that."

"I know. Yesterday morning you were an ordinary workingwoman. You and your son were safe. I'm sorry I brought these people into your life."

She searched his face. "I was so terrified they would kill you," she whispered.

"I'm not going anywhere." He traced the curve of her jaw with his thumb. Her skin was so incredibly soft, yet she was as tough as any man he knew. She had been terrified for her son's safety, yet had found the courage to do whatever it took to save him. Her combination of vulnerability and strength stirred him.

She closed her eyes and leaned into his palm. The

tenderness and sensuality of the gesture fired his senses. He bent, his lips hovering over hers. "If you don't want me to kiss you, you'd better say so now," he murmured.

In answer, she slid her arms around his neck. "Kiss me," she said, and drew him to her.

The attraction he had felt for her flared into the full heat of desire when her lips touched his. Her mouth claimed him, erasing all other thought or sensation. He angled his head to explore her lips more fully, tracing his tongue across the seam, tasting her and feeling her breath hot and silken against his cheek. He caressed the satin of her neck with one hand and slid the other down to the curve of her hip.

Her lips parted and she made a breathy sound of welcome as he deepened the kiss. All the tension and fear of the last hours melted away in the fire of that embrace. He felt lighter and freer than he had in weeks, and when at last she gently pulled away, he found he was smiling.

She returned the smile, shy and maybe a little dazed. "You'd better see to the food," she said. "I'll go wake Ian."

He moved to the stove to turn off the pot of chili, but the memory of her lingered on his skin like warm silk. He hated that he had brought danger into her life, but he couldn't be sorry he had met her. Yes, she had saved his life when she fired on Gravel Voice, but she had rescued him even before that moment.

With Andrea, he could feel himself healing, becoming whole again in a way he had begun to think was out of reach.

Chapter Seven

Andrea stood beside the sofa, staring down at her sleeping child, her lips still tingling from Jack's kiss, her skin pebbled with goose bumps from the loss of his warmth. She had never intended to kiss him. She wasn't a woman who behaved impulsively or who had casual relationships with men. Or any relationships, really. She was a working mother with a son to raise. She didn't have time for all the drama and risk of dating.

But kissing Jack had felt so right. She had grown so close to him in the last two days as they worked together to save her son. When she looked into his eyes, she found no pity or false promises, only a steady faith in her that had melted some of the chill she had carried inside her ever since the night Preston was killed.

Still, she needed to be careful, she reminded herself. She had just met Jack and knew very little about him. With scarcely a second thought, she had trusted her life and that of her son to him, and so far he had proved worthy of that trust. But could she take the next step and trust him with her heart, as well? Every instinct for self-preservation told her to back away and protect herself. But in Jack's arms she wanted nothing more than to surrender to feelings she hadn't allowed herself to experience in years.

"Mommy?" Ian's voice, soft and sleepy, pulled her from her reverie. She hurried to sit beside him.

"I'm right here, baby," she said, rubbing his leg. "Are you hungry? Jack made some chili for us."

"Chili sounds good." He sat up and rubbed his face. "I'm thirsty, too."

"I'm sure we can find something to drink."

"Do we have any root beer?"

She laughed. "I'm afraid not." She stood and leaned down to pick him up, but he slid off the sofa.

"I can walk." Trailing his blanket, he hurried into the kitchen, his feet making soft slapping sounds on the bare floor.

Smiling, she followed. She had to keep reminding herself that he wasn't really a baby anymore. Every day he asserted his own personality more, an odd mixture of hers and Preston's quirks—and new traits that were clearly all his own.

What would Preston think of his son if he could see him now? she wondered. He'd been a good husband during the pregnancy and birth and was proud to be a father, but he wasn't the kind of man who was very involved in child care. He came from a tradition where men provided for and protected their families but women did most of the hands-on parenting.

Jack looked up from ladling chili into bowls when Andrea followed Ian into the kitchen. "Grab a seat and have some chili, buddy," he said.

Ian climbed onto one of the rickety folding chairs. "I like it when you call me buddy," he said.

"That's because you are my buddy." Jack looked up and caught Andrea's eye, and she swallowed the sudden knot in her throat. He was so good with Ian. So natural. She never would have expected that the big tough FBI agent would have such an easy way with kids.

"Do you have brothers and sisters?" she asked as she pulled out the chair across from Ian. "Nieces and nephews?"

"I have a younger sister, but she's still single. Why?"

"You're so good with kids. I just wondered."

"I like kids. Well, maybe not all kids, but I like Ian."

"I like you, too." Ian looked up from crumbling crackers on top of his chili. "How long are we going to stay here?"

"We have to wait until the snow stops and the road is clear," he said. "It could be a while."

"One of the men we overheard said something about a radio," Andrea said. "If we found it, we could listen to the weather report."

"I'll look for it later," Jack said. "I'm going to take the plywood off these windows, too, and let in some light."

"Good idea." She suppressed a shudder and focused on the hot chili. Maybe the cabin wouldn't seem so gloomy without the boarded-up windows.

"How long do we have to stay?" Ian asked, with a child's insistence on specifics.

"The weather report on my phone calls for snow most of the night," Jack said. "Think of it like a sleepover."

Warmth curled through Andrea as she contemplated spending the night in this small cabin with Jack. Of course, they had a five-year-old chaperone to keep anything from happening, but after the kisses they had shared, being near him felt so much more intimate. Now that he'd reminded her that she was a woman with sensual needs, she couldn't seem to think of anything else.

"Just as long as we don't miss Christmas," Ian said.

"Oh, honey." Andrea smoothed the back of his head. "Christmas is over a week away. We won't be here nearly that long." At least, she hoped not.

After their late lunch, Andrea washed dishes while Jack used a pry bar from his truck to remove the plywood from the cabin's side and back windows. "I'm leaving the front boarded up," he said. "So that it doesn't look different to anyone driving in. If anyone returns, I don't want to make it too obvious we're here. I'm going to move my truck behind the cabin, too."

"Having the windows uncovered makes it feel less claustrophobic," she said. "Thank you."

He toweled off his hair, leaving it uncombed and sexy looking. Melted snow beaded on his forearms and a stray droplet rolled down his neck. She had to fight the urge to lick it off.

"Is something wrong?" he asked. He put a hand to his neck. "Did I get mud on me or something?"

She turned away, her face burning. "Can I borrow your phone?" she asked. "I need to call my office and let my assistant know what's going on."

Though she had left a message early this morning that she wouldn't be in today, she told Stacy to cancel tomorrow's appointments as well, once she got in touch with her. "Is everything okay?" the assistant asked. "Is there anything I can do?"

"Everything is going to be fine. I just had a family emergency that I need to take care of. There's nothing you can do. I should be back tomorrow afternoon or the next day." Surely the snow would have stopped by then.

"Be careful traveling," the assistant said. "The weather is awful and a lot of roads are closed, including most of the mountain passes."

She ended the call, then phoned Chelsea. "Are you

all right?" her friend asked after she had answered on the first ring. "Is Ian okay?"

"Ian is fine. We're both fine. Ian, do you want to say hello to Chelsea?"

"Hello, Chelsea." Ian sat on a quilt in front of the woodstove with Jack, who was showing him how to make a "telephone" with the two washed-out chili cans and a piece of string he'd unearthed in a kitchen drawer.

"What happened?" Chelsea asked. "If I didn't hear from you soon, I was going to call the police."

"It's okay," Andrea said. "Jack and I found Ian at the address the kidnappers gave us and they ended up running away." She saw no need to mention the dead man or the frightening race to the river.

"That's it? They just ran away?"

"Well…it was a little more complicated than that, but the main thing is, we're all right and they're gone. How are you doing?"

"I have a headache and I'm still a little shook up, but I'll be fine. Will you be home soon?"

"That's one of the reasons I called. All this snow means the roads into this fishing camp are impassable. We won't be able to leave until the snow stops and the county plows clear the way."

"Where did you say you are?" Chelsea asked.

"It's a fishing camp—a bunch of cabins on the banks of the Pine River, outside Bayfield. We've moved into one of them. It's dry and there's a woodstove and we have food. Not gourmet, but we'll be fine."

"So you're spending the night there?" Chelsea asked. "With Jack?"

"And Ian."

"Uh-huh. Well, the kid has to sleep sometime. And a cabin in the woods with the snow outside and a nice fire inside sounds pretty romantic to me."

"Chelsea!" Andrea would have protested that she scarcely knew Jack and she didn't think of him that way. But Jack was sitting only a few feet away. And the humming in her body whenever he was near told her that she did indeed think of Jack "that way."

Chelsea laughed. "Hey, he's gorgeous and he seems really into you. I say go for it. A guy who will go out of his way like that for you and your son is a keeper."

Her heart fluttered at the words and she looked across the room at Jack, who was patiently showing Ian how to knot the string so that it wouldn't slip out of the can. "It's too soon to tell," she said.

"Coward," Chelsea said. "Trust me, you don't forget how to have sex just because you haven't had it in a while."

"Uh-huh. I have to go now, Chelsea."

"I want a full report when you get home." Laughing, Chelsea ended the call.

"Here's your phone." She crossed the room and returned it to Jack.

"We made a phone, Mom. Look." Ian giggled and put the empty chili can to his ear. "Hello. Mr. Jack, can you hear me?"

Jack peered from around the kitchen door and spoke into his chili can. "Hey, Mr. Ian. How are things at your end of the room?"

"My mom wants to talk to you." Ian thrust the can into Andrea's hand. "Say hello, Mama."

"Hello, Jack."

"Mom! You have to talk into the phone."

Andrea nodded and moved the can to her mouth. "Hello?"

Jack said something she couldn't make out. Ian erupted in giggles. "Mom! Now you have to put the phone to your ear."

Sheepish, she moved the can to her ear. "You're the sexiest playmate I ever had." The words, issued in a low, masculine whisper, sent heat to more than just her face.

"I want to talk now," Ian said, and reclaimed the can.

Andrea curled up on the sofa and watched her son and Jack play. The telephone call morphed into a mock wrestling match, which ended with Jack giving Ian a ride on his shoulders all through the cabin while they both sang loudly, and off-key, a song with made-up lyrics about slaying monsters.

Jack had slain Ian's monsters, turning this cabin from a place of fear into a place of fun. He had beaten back some of Andrea's fear, too, though she needed to hold on to some of it for a little longer. Some of her fears—of letting go or giving in, of trusting someone else with her happiness—had kept her going in the years since Preston's death. She couldn't afford to give that up just yet.

The warm fire and her son's happy laughter lulled her into a doze there on the sofa. When she woke, someone—probably Jack—had covered her with a blanket. He sat in the cabin's one armchair across from her, Ian on his lap, both of them studying something on his phone. "How long have I been sleeping?" she asked, sitting up and raking a hand through her hair.

"A long time," Ian said.

"A couple of hours." Jack's smile was like a caress, sending a rush of pleasure through her.

"Jack and me have been playing games on his phone," Ian said.

"Jack and I," she automatically corrected, worry raising its familiar head as she came more fully awake. As much as she loved seeing Ian so happy, she knew he would be crushed when Jack left. And Jack would leave. His job would take him away from them, both physically and mentally. One of the great disappointments of her marriage had been discovering that even when Preston was with her, part of him was focused on criminals and clues and the work that consumed him.

"I'm hungry," Ian announced.

"I'm hungry, too." Jack stood, lifting the boy with him. "Let's go see what we can rustle up for dinner, bud."

Andrea retreated to the bathroom, where she frowned at the sleep marks on her face and the tangles in her hair. She wasn't exactly a sexy playmate now. And it was just as well. As flattering as it was for Jack to see her that way, it wasn't a good idea if she intended to keep her distance. No sense starting something with him that would only end badly.

Dinner was canned beef stew and biscuits from a mix Jack found in the cupboard. "Jack is a good cook," Ian announced, beaming at his new best friend.

"I'm sure your mom does a much better job," Jack said.

"But she always makes vegetables and fish and stuff." Ian made a face. "Healthy food."

Jack laughed and winked at Andrea. She looked away.

After supper she helped Jack clear the table. "You cooked, so I can do the dishes," she said.

"We'll do them together." He took out his phone and handed it to Ian. "Hey, buddy. Why don't you go play in the other room while your mom and I clean up in here."

Ian took the phone. "I wanna play with you," he said. "Mom can do the dishes by herself."

"Ian McNeil," Andrea said. "You've monopolized Jack all afternoon. You can play by yourself for a little bit."

"Okay." With all the reluctance and drama of a stubborn five-year-old, he shuffled out of the room.

Andrea began gathering up the plates, scraping them into the garbage can under the sink. Jack filled the basin with hot, soapy water. "He's a great kid," he said.

"Yes, he is."

"I think he's going to bounce back pretty well from this." He took the plates from her and slid them into the water.

"I have a colleague who specializes in children's issues. I'll probably have her talk to him, just to be sure he's okay." She picked up a dish towel and stepped to one side to make more room for him at the sink.

"That sounds like a good idea." He handed her the first clean plate.

"I'm sorry you're stuck here with us," she said. "I mean, I'm not sorry you're with us, but I regret that we've intruded on your life this way."

"I thought I'd made it clear that I don't see you as an intrusion." He scrubbed at dried food in a pan. "Besides, I'm on medical leave. My days were full of bad TV and too much brooding about whatever was going on with the case without me."

"That must be frustrating," she said. "Being involved in an investigation for months, then suddenly finding yourself left out."

"It is." He paused, both hands immersed in the soapy water. "Being here makes me feel less useless, at least. And though I haven't found a solid connection yet, I'm sure the people who took Ian are connected to the men I'm hunting."

"Maybe the Bureau's investigators will find the connection when they search the camp."

"Maybe." He began rinsing the next dish. "But they'll just shut me out again. If I found the connection myself—the proof that what happened to you and Ian is linked to Braeswood and his activities— they would have a tougher time excluding me, medical leave or not."

He sounded so wistful, frustration clear in the set of his jaw and the tension in his shoulders. She put a comforting hand on his arm. "I hope you find what you need," she said. "I'd help you if I knew what to look for."

"Thanks." His gaze met hers, and she felt a renewed rush of pleasure—and uneasiness. She was still so unsure of where the two of them were headed. She looked away and pretended to focus on drying a plate.

"What's wrong?" he asked. "Are you worried about what's going to happen tomorrow?"

She hadn't even let herself think about tomorrow yet. "What is going to happen?" she asked.

"As soon it's safe to travel, we can leave. The Bureau is sending a team out to take this place apart. At some point, they'll want to interview you about what happened."

She fumbled the plate she was drying. He put a steadying hand on her wrist. "Don't worry. You're not in any kind of trouble. They just want to gather as much information as they can in order to find these guys."

She slid her hand from his grasp and focused on drying the plate. "Do you think those men will try to go after Ian again?" The possibility made her feel sick.

"I doubt it. But in case they do, I'm not leaving your side until this is settled."

She looked up, alarmed. "You don't have to do that."

"I'm officially on medical leave, so I don't have any other pressing duties. And it's my fault this happened in the first place. I'm going to make sure they don't have a chance to hurt you again."

She believed he could protect her and her son, and knowing he was watching over them would probably make her feel much safer. But spending more days or even weeks in close proximity to him could cause all kinds of other problems. Ian would grow even more attached to him and she…she would grow more attached to him, too. She rubbed the dish in her hand so hard it squeaked. "I'm sure we'll be fine

on our own. I can always call the police if I see anything suspicious."

He let the dishrag slide into the water. "What's
wrong?" he asked. The dampness from his hands
soaked into her shirt as he gripped her shoulders.

She shrugged away from him. Everything was
wrong. She and Ian shouldn't even be here. They
should be home, on a normal night after work, eating a meal she had cooked and getting ready for his
bedtime story. "Nothing's wrong," she lied.

He released her but didn't return to washing
dishes. "Something has upset you," he said. "Something to do with me. What is it?"

She tossed the dish towel onto the counter and
faced him. Maybe he was right. Maybe they did need
to talk about this. "I'm worried about what's going
to happen to Ian when you leave," she said. "He's
clearly crazy about you."

"What about you?" His gaze searched her face.
"How do you feel about me?"

"How I feel doesn't matter. I have to think of my
son."

"We've already established that Ian likes me. I
want to know how *you* feel about me." He took a
step closer, crowding her against the counter but not
quite touching her. "When we were kissing earlier,
I got the impression you thought I was okay." His
voice was low, rough with emotion, sending a shiver
across her skin.

She folded her arms across her chest. "That kiss was a mistake. Yes, I'm attracted to you, but…"

"But what?" He cupped her chin in his hand, and she leaned into his touch, in spite of her determination not to. "Do you think because you're a mother, you don't get to act on your feelings?" he asked.

"If I let you get closer to me, it's only going to hurt Ian when you leave." *And it's going to hurt me, too. I don't want to deal with any more pain.*

He slid his hand down her neck and moved nearer, the front of his shirt brushing her breasts, his eyes dark with desire, mesmerizing her. "Who says I'm leaving?" He kissed her cheek, a feather brush against her sensitive nerves.

"You have a job to go back to." She forced herself to focus on the issue at hand, to ignore her racing heart and the tension building inside her.

"So do you," he said, and kissed her other cheek.

She put her hands up to push him away but only rested her palms against the hard plane of his chest. She fixed her gaze on him, stern and determined. "Your job is different," she said. "Police work is— It's consuming. It's not something you can leave behind at the end of the day."

He leaned back, his mouth set in a hard line. "You mean it's not something your husband could leave behind. I'm not him."

"I counsel plenty of law enforcement officers,"

she said. "One of the traits of the good ones is that they're very focused."

"In your work, I'm guessing one of the things you work on with people is balance," he said. "You help your clients find that equilibrium between work and the rest of their life."

She nodded. "It's a common problem for law enforcement."

"It's a common problem for everyone. But no life is ever perfectly balanced. Sometimes the scales tip more toward work. When I'm on an important case, I have to put in long hours and devote a lot of my attention to the job. What I'm doing is important to the safety of the country. To the safety of people like you and Ian."

"I realize that. But I also know that you came to me because you couldn't let go of your guilt over your colleague's death. Something that happened on the job was affecting every aspect of your life."

"One reason that happened, I think, is because the job, and the friendships I've made there, were all I had in my life. At the end of the day I came home to an empty apartment. I didn't have anyone else who mattered to me. Now I do."

Her therapist's training had taught her to read between the lines of what her clients told her, and to pick up on subtle cues of body language to divine their feelings. But she didn't trust her instincts when it came to Jack. "What are you saying?" she asked.

"I'm saying that you and Ian have become important to me. I had this void in my life and you two have moved in to fill it up." He cradled the back of her head, fingers threaded into her hair. "I know we haven't known each other long, but from the moment I met you, I felt a connection. It was as if I had been looking for you and I hadn't even realized it until I found you."

"I felt the connection, too." She curled her fingers against him, no longer pushing him away but reluctant to pull him to her. "It caught me off guard. I don't know what to think. I…I don't want to lose you."

"Life is all about risk." He moved his hands to her shoulders again, reassuring and gentle. "Relationships are never easy. But I think the two of us are smart enough to figure this out. I want to try."

Instinct told her to shy away from complications she didn't need, but a small voice in her head—or maybe from her heart—told her she would be a fool to pass up a chance with a man with whom she had felt such an immediate connection. "Maybe we could try," she said.

"You're right about one thing," he said. "I am focused. When I'm at work, I'm focused on work. And when I'm with you, I'm very focused on you." He tipped her head up, his gaze fixed on her mouth, which tingled as if he had touched her.

She wet her lips and tried and failed to draw

a steady breath. He was like a tide, pulling her under, and when he bent to her, she closed her eyes and surrendered.

Chapter Eight

Andrea had expected a repeat of their earlier kiss, forceful and almost overwhelming in its passion. Instead, Jack teased her with the slightest brush of his lips against hers. Then he trailed a line of similarly gentle caresses along her jaw until his mouth rested against the pulse at the base of her throat. Her body hummed with awareness, every nerve attuned to the heat and strength and *maleness* of him.

She gripped his biceps and arched to him, the sensitive tips of her breasts pressed into his muscular chest. "What are you doing to me?" she whispered.

"I want you." He nipped at her neck, just beneath her ear, his words as much as his touch sending a tremor through her. "But I don't want to rush you. We've got all night. Or longer, if you need it."

All she needed right now was him. All her fears and worries seemed petty in the face of that fundamental longing. Tomorrow or the next day or next week or next month he might leave her, but tonight they were together, and she knew if she pushed him away now, she would regret it for the rest of her life. She rose on tiptoe and pressed her lips to his. "Let me check on Ian," she said.

He followed her into the cabin's front room, where they found Ian asleep on the sofa, curled on his side, Jack's phone still in his hand. Jack retrieved the phone, then added wood to the fire while Andrea covered her son with a blanket. Then Jack took her hand and led her into the bedroom. "We'll hear him if he wakes," he said.

"He probably won't even stir," she said. "He's always been a hard sleeper. Nothing to trouble his dreams, I guess." Unlike her. Many of her nights were restless.

"Does he miss his father?" Jack asked.

His genuine concern for the boy touched her. "I don't think he really remembers Preston. I keep his picture in Ian's room and Ian asks about him sometimes, but the way he might ask me about an actor on TV or a character in his favorite storybook. Now that he's in school and he hears other children talk about their dads, I think he's more curious about the idea of a father." Some of those conversations were so painful, trying to explain to Ian why other boys had fathers and he didn't.

Jack massaged the back of her neck, kneading at the knotted muscles. "Do you miss Preston?"

"Sometimes." She let out a deep breath, trying to release the tension inside her, too. "I miss what we had when we first married. That sense of being the most important person in the world to someone else. Later on, after he made detective and joined the drug task force, we lost some of that closeness. I felt as if Ian and I only got whatever energy Preston had left over from the job."

"The job has a way of sucking some people in," he said. "The excitement and the feeling that you're making a difference can be a real rush. Home life can seem dull in comparison."

"I'm not blaming him," she said. "I expected too much of him sometimes and didn't try hard enough to see things from his perspective. Counseling other spouses of law enforcement officers has taught me so much. It's the regrets that trouble me now more than the grief."

He put his arms around her and pulled her close. She welcomed the embrace and laid her head on his chest, the steady beat of his heart a calming rhythm. "I think whenever a relationship ends unexpectedly, we try to understand and cope by playing that what-if game," he said. "What if I had said this or done that or not done or said those other things?" His lips brushed the top of her head. "But that's a game you can't win. You can't change the past."

"So I'm fond of telling my clients." She pulled away enough to look up at him. "I also tell them they can't control the future, so it's important to focus on the now."

"That word again. *Focus.*" He slid his hands down to rest at the small of her back, pulling her tight against him. The hard ridge of his erection nudged at her belly, leaving no doubt of his feelings for her. "I can think of a few things I'd like to focus on right now."

"Oh?"

"I'd like to focus here." He slid one hand up to stroke the side of her breast, sending ripples of pleasure through her. "Or here." He arched against her, letting her feel the evidence of his desire. "And here." He slid his thigh between her legs, pressing against the center of her arousal.

"Those...those all sound like good ideas," she gasped. She pulled his head down and found his lips, blotting out her nervousness with a long, drugging kiss. Then he was pulling her down onto the mattress, laying her back and half covering her with his body. The bed was made now, with fresh sheets and blankets. Jack must have done this, perhaps while she was napping on the sofa. Was it because he'd planned to bring her here later, or merely because he had wanted a comfortable bed for the night?

And then the answer didn't matter as he slid his hand beneath the sweatshirt, reclaiming her full attention. He skimmed his hand up her thigh and over her stomach to caress her breast. She tugged at his shirt until he lifted enough for her to push it up so that she could run her hands over the smooth muscles of his abdomen and chest. A fine dusting of hair tickled her palms as she traced the outline of his pecs, and his nipples pebbled at her touch.

He sat up and removed his shirt, then helped her out of hers, as well. His gaze lingered on her so long she began to feel self-conscious, and she tried to cross her arms over her breasts, but he pulled her hands away. "You're beautiful," he said. "So beautiful," he murmured again as he bent and drew one taut peak into his mouth.

Desire lanced through her, sharp and urgent. She bit her knuckle to stifle her cry and bowed her body against him. He slid his hand under her back, pulling her closer, and transferred his attention to her other breast. To be held this way, so intimately and tenderly, after too many years alone made her eyes burn with threatening tears. Then he raked his teeth across her sensitive nipple and any lingering sadness fled. Skimming her hand down his torso, she fumbled for the drawstring of his sweat pants, aware of the hard length of him straining at the fabric.

He shoved her hand out of the way and slid back from her long enough to strip off his pants, then removed her panties, as well. She gasped at the rush of cool air across her naked flesh and then he was beside her once more, cupping between her legs, one finger parting her folds, his touch warming and exciting her until she was panting with need.

She reached for him, wrapping her fingers around

his erection and smiling when his breath caught. "Don't make me wait any longer," she said.

In answer, he pushed onto his knees and reached for his gym bag beside the bed. He pulled out a condom package. She laughed. "Do you always travel so prepared?" she asked.

"This has probably been in there for years," he said. "From the days when I was either a little more active or maybe just more optimistic."

She was prepared to tease him more, but he ripped open the package and sheathed himself. Watching him made her mouth grow dry and she lost the power of speech. He arched over her, kneeling between her legs. "Are you ready?" he asked, caressing her hip.

"So ready," she breathed, and opened to welcome him in.

The intensity of his passion didn't surprise her, for it matched the power of her own need. But the tenderness with which he touched her moved her even more, as if he cherished as much as desired her. They began slowly, savoring the feel of each other's bodies, hands and mouths continuing to explore and excite.

But they could hold back only so long and soon they were moving in an urgent rhythm, one that was both familiar and brand-new. Her last nervousness vanished and she began a quick climb toward a climax that overwhelmed her with its intensity. The shock waves of her orgasm were still moving through her when he found his own release, and they clung to each other tightly for long moments afterward, until their heartbeats slowed and they came back to themselves.

He lay beside her, her head pillowed in the hollow of his shoulder. This, too, felt so right and comfortable. She had known Preston for over a year before she'd felt this comfortable with him. Was that only because she had been younger then, or was it because of Jack himself?

"What are you thinking?" he asked, gently squeezing her shoulder.

"Do you know why I agreed to go to lunch with you the other day?" she asked.

"Because of my good looks and charm?"

"Well, that may have had something to do with it, but it's not the main reason."

"What's the main reason, then?"

"You said you thought I would be good company." Did that confession make her sound pathetic? She plunged on. "You didn't try to flatter me by complimenting my looks or telling me what good company *you'd* be. You made me believe you thought I was worth listening to."

His arm tightened around her. "I do believe that," he said. "Do you know why I asked you to lunch?"

"You said it was because you were bored and lonely." She had to admit that had helped persuade her, too—nothing like a big, strong guy being a little vulnerable.

"I was. But it was more that in the hour we spent together in your office, I sensed a connection. Something that wasn't just about a doctor-patient relationship. I hadn't felt that with a woman before and I wanted to experience it a little longer and see where it went."

And they had ended up here, in bed together, though the route they had taken to get here was anything but conventional. "Being with you is easy for me," she said. "I can't say that about any other man I've met lately. Maybe it's because you're a good listener."

"Not always. But I like looking at you *and* listening to you."

She liked listening to him, too, and thought—maybe—he might be a man she never tired of listening to. That was a good start for a relationship, right? She'd have to see if she felt the same way when her and Ian's lives were no longer in danger, when Jack wasn't merely their best protection, but a man she wanted in her life as much as she needed him.

JACK WOKE BEFORE DAWN, the warm weight of Andrea curled beside him already familiar and right. In the midst of such a crazy, dangerous situation, he felt more at peace with her than he had in months. The soft sigh of her breathing was the only sound in the early-morning quiet. A glance toward the window showed a swath of pale blue sky, with no sign of storm clouds. Careful not to wake her, he eased out of bed and began to dress.

He slipped into the kitchen to make coffee, and when he returned from the bathroom to retrieve his shoes, she was sitting up in bed, the covers pulled up over her chest, a sleepy smile on her face. "Do you always get up this early?" she asked, her voice soft and quiet.

"The snow has stopped and plows should clear the road soon." He pulled on his shirt and began buttoning it. "I want to search the camp before we have to leave."

She drew up her knees and hugged them to her chest. "I thought you said the Bureau is sending in a team this afternoon to search."

"They are. But I want to see if I can find anything first." He knelt to tie the laces of his shoes. "I won't be long."

"Be careful," she said. "Preston used to tell stories about drug dealers and smugglers booby-trapping their hideouts. And that netting I was caught in may not be the worst trap Anderson and his buddies set."

"I will." He bent to kiss her. She slid her hand around his neck and pulled him close when he tried to move away. Desire heated his blood once more. "You're tempting me to stay," he murmured, nibbling at the side of her mouth.

"I just wanted to give you something to think about while you were gone." She smiled, then released him with a show of reluctance. "I know a little boy who's probably going to wake up soon, so I'd better be there for him when he does."

"I'll definitely be thinking about you." He rose and left the room, stopping in the kitchen to pour the coffee. As he worked, he heard her come out of the bedroom.

"Hi, Mama," a sleepy voice greeted her.

"Did you sleep well, pumpkin?" she asked.

"Uh-huh. Is Jack still here?"

"I'm here, buddy." A cup of coffee in each hand, Jack moved into the living room. He handed one cup to Andrea and sipped from the other. "I'm going out to check on a few things," he told Ian. "I'll be back in a minute."

"Can I go with you?" Ian asked.

"Not right now. Somebody has to stay here with your mom." He ruffled the boy's hair. "I'll be back in time for breakfast."

Ian looked as if he wanted to argue, but Andrea said, "Let's go brush your teeth and then you can help me decide what to cook for breakfast."

Jack stepped out into sharp air, heavy with the scents of ponderosa pine and wood smoke. The sun was sending its first rays over the tops of the trees, revealing buildings shrouded in snow, their outlines softened and the drabness disguised by the cloak of winter white. He tried to imagine what the camp must have looked like in its heyday, with waderclad fishermen gathering to cast their flies for the rainbow and brown trout that populated the river behind the cabins. He'd like to come back here to fish one day, maybe with Ian in tow. Jack would show the boy how to choose a fly and cast into the deep pools where the trout liked to linger. Andrea would be in the scene, too, perhaps with a younger child in her arms...

Where had that come from? He shook off the daydream and drained the coffee cup, then set it on the porch railing. He and Andrea and the boy needed to leave right after breakfast in case Anderson and his men elected to come back with reinforcements. He decided to start in the ruins of the office. The group appeared to have been using it as some kind of headquarters, and he hoped to find a safe or something in the ashes that might give a clue to their purpose here beyond holding Ian hostage.

Snow crunched under his boots as he made his way across the compound, and the bitter smell of char and ash stung his nose as he approached the ruins. He played the beam of his flashlight over the charred timbers and blackened plumbing. Careful not to disturb the scene, he moved to the front room, where Gravel Voice had been shot, but found no sign of a body. Springs from the sofa and the wheels of an office chair jutted up from the debris, but there was no sign of the dead man. If he had, indeed, died.

Had Anderson and Leo taken their boss with them

when they left? Maybe the man's identity would provide a link to them that they didn't want authorities to discover. If so, he hadn't followed them out of the car when it stalled on the bridge. Jack would have to alert the team to look for it.

He didn't spot a safe or anything else useful in the burned-out ruins, so he moved on to the first cabin in the semicircle. Though he had briefly explored all the buildings yesterday after they had returned to camp, this morning he wanted to take a closer look to see if he could unearth more evidence. Special Agent in Charge Blessing would have lectured him on the need to wait for the professional evidence team, but Jack didn't want to lose his chance to be a vital part of the investigation again. Once he and Andrea left here, he had more weeks of medical leave that would put him further and further out of the loop. If he found important clues today, he'd have more leverage when it came to being included in updates about the investigation.

He worked his way down the row of cabins. All of them were unlocked, and the first two appeared to have been unoccupied for years, dust thick on the tops of tables and windowsills. A pack rat had built a nest in the bedroom of one, a massive, messy pile full of scraps of paper, bent silverware and old fishing lures. Definitely let the pros tackle that mess. For now, he wanted a better look at the cabin where Anderson had been staying.

Like the others in the camp, Anderson's cabin, in the middle of the semicircle, was a simple plank-sided structure with a small front porch and a bedroom, bathroom and kitchen lined up behind a larger front room. As Jack stepped into the front room, a mouse skittered away from an open bag of potato chips that lay on the floor by one of the armchairs.

The kitchen yielded only dirty dishes piled in the sink, the refrigerator stocked with cold cuts and cheap beer. The bathroom held only a towel and a used disposable razor. Jack moved on to the bedroom. Like the rest of the cabin, it was in disarray, bedclothes trailing to the floor, dresser drawers half-open to reveal a few T-shirts and some underwear and socks. Studying the scene, Jack felt the hair on the back of his neck stand on end. There was something important here, he sensed. Something he needed to see.

He tugged the blanket the rest of the way off the bed, then pulled off the sheet and tossed it aside, too. Unlike the mattress on the floor in the cabin where he had spent the night, this room contained an iron bed frame with a mattress and box spring. Jack bent and shone his light beneath the frame. Something dark and bulky was shoved far back, against the wall.

He had to lie on his stomach to retrieve the item, which proved to be a backpack—the kind used by hikers and campers. It looked fairly new and unworn, so he doubted it had been forgotten by some long-ago visitor to the camp.

He deposited the pack on the mattress and unzipped the main compartment. His light revealed a handgun, a cigarette lighter, a spiral notebook and a sheaf of papers bound together with a rubber band. Definitely worth checking out. He slung the pack over one shoulder and left the building.

Andrea greeted him at the door of the end cabin when he worked his way back to it. "I was getting a little worried," she said.

"No worries." He kissed her cheek, surprised by how good it felt to have someone worry about him and welcome him back. He'd always dismissed such sentiments as unimportant, but now he saw he'd been wrong. Whereas before, the mission had been the most important thing in his mind, now coming home after the work was done was also a priority.

"Where did you get the backpack?" she asked as he moved past her into the cabin.

"I found it in the cabin where Anderson was staying. I didn't see it yesterday, because it was under the bed. I thought I'd bring it in here for a closer look."

"Breakfast is ready. Oatmeal and canned peaches. Ian insisted we wait for you before we ate." She started to lead the way to the kitchen, but he took her arm, stopping her.

"I checked the burned-out office," he said, keeping his voice low, not wanting the boy to overhear. "The man you shot isn't there."

Confusion clouded her eyes. "Did he...did he burn up in the fire?"

"I don't think so. Either he got out alive or Anderson and the others took his body with them when they left."

She pressed her lips together and nodded. "Okay. Thanks for letting me know. I was kind of dreading driving past there in daylight."

He squeezed her shoulder. "It's going to be okay," he said. "Let's go have some breakfast."

"There you are," Ian greeted Jack when he entered the room. "Let's eat. I'm hungry."

Jack set the backpack on the floor by his chair and ate the oatmeal and peaches without really tasting them. His mind was focused on the day ahead. He needed to get Ian and Andrea home and check in with his team to find out what they had learned about Anderson and his associates.

When they were finished eating and the table was cleared, Andrea sent Ian to wash up and Jack hefted the backpack onto the table and unpacked its contents. He set aside the lighter, the gun and a clip of ammunition and pulled out the spiral notebook and the sheaf of papers. Men's clothing, a pair of binoculars and half a dozen protein bars filled the rest of the bag.

Jack flipped through the notebook. Andrea moved

from the sink to look over his shoulder. "What's in it?" she asked.

"It looks like mathematical or scientific formulas or something." He passed it to her and she studied the rows of cramped handwriting, then returned it to him.

"It doesn't mean anything to me," she said.

"Maybe it's a code." He put the notebook back into the pack with the clothing, binoculars and the gun. Then he turned his attention to the sheaf of papers. He slipped off the rubber band and studied the first item in the pile.

"Is it a blueprint of some kind?" Andrea asked.

"I think it's a survey, or a plat for a piece of land." He studied the blue lines traced on the page and notations of longitude and latitude. "Somewhere called Center Line Gulch. Have you ever heard of it?"

"No."

He set the paper aside and selected the next page in the bundle, a legal-sized photocopy. This one was easier to decipher. "It's a map," he said. He studied the network of roads and waterways. "There's nothing to indicate where it's from and a lot of the roads aren't marked. It looks like it was photocopied from a larger map or a book."

She leaned forward to peer at the map upside down. "I think it has to be in Colorado," she said. "And this part of the state." She put her finger on a thin line running through the middle of the map. "Doesn't that say Pine River?"

"Yes. And this road has a number." He placed his finger an inch below hers on the map. "Four eighty-seven. I think that's the Forest Service number for the road we're on."

"Then that means we're about here." She tapped the intersection of the river and the road, then slid her finger to the inked circle at the top of the page. "So this has to be fairly nearby."

"Except none of these roads appear to have numbers or names," he said. "They might even be hiking trails, they're so small and faint. There's no legend or scale to indicate the mileage between points."

She squinted at the tiny print on the map. "Nothing on here looks familiar," she said. "I need more context."

He set the map aside. The next item in the pile wasn't a single sheet of paper, but a pamphlet.

"Is that…Russian?" Andrea squinted at the printing on the front of the booklet.

"I think it is." Jack flipped through the booklet but could make no sense of the Cyrillic lettering. He set it aside.

The last item in the pile appeared to be a laboratory report of some kind, detailing the percentage of different minerals found in a core sample. Jack's gaze zeroed in on the word *uranium*. Andrea noticed it, too. "They mine uranium in Colorado," she said. "Or at least, they used to."

He returned the papers to the backpack. "We'll have to dig deeper into this and see if we can figure out what it means. For now, let's hurry up and get out of here. I'll take you and Ian back to your home and coordinate with my team from there."

Ian skipped into the room. "Will you take me to see the creek, Jack?" he asked.

"No time for that, buddy." Jack clapped him on the back. "We're going back to your house."

"Are you coming with us?" Jack asked.

"Yes, I am."

It took only a few minutes to load into Jack's truck. Andrea wanted to straighten the cabin before they left, but he persuaded her not to bother. "The evidence techs are going to tear everything apart anyway," he said.

"I guess you're right," she said. "It just feels so wrong leaving dirty dishes in the sink and the bed unmade."

"Think of it as a good exercise in letting go," he said, steering her toward the truck.

Ian sat belted in the backseat this time, after Jack cleared out a space for him. None of them said anything as they left the camp, although Andrea averted her eyes when they passed the burned-out office building. No other traffic traveled the dirt road leading to the highway. "Do you think the car is still at the second bridge?" Andrea asked, her voice tense.

"If it is, we'll have to move it so we can cross," he said.

"Can you do that?" she asked.

"I have some tow chains in the back."

But there was no sign of the car as they approached the bridge. And little sign of the bridge, either. Snow filled it to the railings, and the road beyond was merely a faint depression in the drifts. "The plows haven't made it here yet," Andrea said.

"No." This wasn't good news. The more time passed, the more chance Anderson and the others had to get away.

"How are we gonna get across?" Ian asked.

Andrea looked at Jack, the same question unspoken in her eyes. He stared at the expanse of white. Even on his own, he wouldn't have wanted to attempt to hike out across that. "We have to go back to the camp," he said. "I'll call my office and see if they can send help."

Andrea said nothing as they returned to camp, though her face was pale and she gripped the edge of the seat, white-knuckled. Jack parked in front of the cabin they had just left and they filed inside. Andrea sank to the sofa and Ian crawled up beside her. "What are we going to do now, Mama?" he asked.

"We're going to sit here quietly while Jack makes a phone call," she said.

He punched in the special agent in charge's private number. "Blessing," the bass voice answered.

"Jack Prescott. I've got a problem."

"What's the problem? Where are you?"

"I'm still at the fishing camp. The snow has stopped but the road is still blocked. We need some help getting out of here."

"Are you or Dr. McNeil or her son hurt or in danger?"

"No." At least with the roads closed, Anderson and his crew weren't likely to return to cause trouble.

"I'll get in touch with local law enforcement," Agent Blessing said. "They should have a better idea of the plowing schedule. But it may be a few hours before they get out there."

"I understand. Give them this number. Any word on Anderson and the other two men I described?"

"We think one of them, the dead man, may be a con named Jerry Altenhaus. He's a small-time extortionist who celled with Anderson for a while about ten years ago. They've been spotted together a few times. No idea who the third man is."

"What about their link to Duane Braeswood?"

"The only one we can tie is Anderson."

"Any word on Braeswood?"

"Agent Prescott, you are still on medical leave."

"I'm still part of your team," Jack said.

Blessing made a sound that was a cross between a sigh and a groan. "We have a lead on Braeswood that we're investigating. At this point, we're pretty sure he's still alive and active."

"I did a brief search of the camp and found a back-pack with some documents that may be relevant," Jack said. "I'll bring them with me when we get out of here and Forensics can see if they can make anything of them."

"Anything else I need to know?" Blessing asked.

Jack glanced toward the sofa, but Ian and Andrea were intent on a game of tic-tac-toe, scribbled on a scrap of paper she had found on the coffee table. He lowered his voice. "The man who we shot—his body isn't here. I don't know if Anderson and his companion carried it with them when they left or if he got up and walked out on his own. I don't think it likely. He was shot point-blank in the back with a .44-caliber pistol."

"In the back?" Blessing's voice was sharp.

"He was about to shoot me when Andrea—Dr. McNeil—shot him."

"This will all be in your report."

"Yes, sir." Jack resisted the urge to argue that if he was well enough to write reports, he ought to be allowed to return to work.

"Jack?"

The strain in Andrea's voice, and the deathly pallor of her face when he turned to look at her, put Jack on high alert. "Sir, I have to go," he said.

"Sit tight and stay out of trouble," Blessing said. "I'll be in touch."

Jack pocketed the phone and moved to Andrea's side. "What's wrong?" he asked, taking her hand.

With a warning glance toward Ian, who knelt at the coffee table, scribbling something on a scrap of paper, Andrea pulled Jack toward the kitchen. He could feel her trembling as they stepped into the room. "What is it?" he asked again. "You're shaking like a leaf."

"Someone was here while we were gone," she said. "Someone came into the cabin." Her eyes met his, a mixture of fear and anger reflected in their dark depths. "We're not alone anymore, Jack. And I've got a very bad feeling about this."

Chapter Nine

Jack reached inside his jacket to check the pistol in his shoulder holster. "Why do you think someone was in here?" he asked.

She pointed to the kitchen table, cluttered with the remains of their breakfast. "There was still some oatmeal in a pot on the stove when we left," she said. "It's gone. A can of milk and some crackers are missing from the cabinets, too. I came in here to make some cocoa and peanut butter crackers for Ian and I couldn't find them."

"Maybe some homeless person was looking for food." The words didn't even sound convincing to Jack.

"This isn't the city," she said. "This is the middle of nowhere. If a homeless person was around here, why not just move into one of the empty cabins? Why wait until we drove away and come into this one?" She gripped his hand, her fingernails digging into his palms. "Do you think it's the man I shot?"

"Andrea, there's no way he's still alive," Jack said. "You shot him at close range. I saw the exit wound."

"Then where is his body?"

"It's probably still in that car, buried in the snow on the bridge. Anderson and his partner probably took the body with them to delay having it identified and linked to them. Besides, if it was him, why wouldn't he have gone to the first cabin and retrieved the backpack? A weapon would be more use to him than oatmeal and canned milk." He stared at the clutter on the table. "None of this makes sense."

"What did your boss say about getting us out of here?" she asked.

"He's going to contact local law enforcement and see if they can get the plows out here to clear the road for us. He's going to call me back."

She rubbed her hands up and down her arms, as if she had a chill. "I hope they hurry. Whether this is a vagrant or one of the kidnappers on the loose, I don't want to be anywhere near those people."

"Neither do I." He walked to the window and checked the latch. "In the meantime, I'll find some nails and make sure no one can come in the windows. And we'll keep the door locked." That wouldn't be much defense against a high-powered rifle, but no sense worrying her further by mentioning that. Besides, he still wasn't convinced their thief had anything to do with the terrorists. "It was probably a kid thinking they were getting away with something," he said. "Try not to worry about it."

"I've always thought that was some of the most pointless advice in the English language," she said. She moved to the sink and began running water. "Considering the events of the last forty-eight hours, only a fool wouldn't worry."

"I know you're not a fool." He started to go to her but thought better of it. She didn't want comfort right now; she wanted action. "I'll take care of those windows," he said. "And if anyone comes back, I'll be ready for them."

PUTTING THE KITCHEN in order helped Andrea feel a little calmer. Now that she had had time to process what had happened, it was hard to be afraid of some- one who was desperate enough to steal cold oatmeal and canned milk. But the idea that someone else was out there, watching them, gave her the creeps.

The kitchen cabinets didn't contain much in the way of food beyond canned staples, but she un- earthed a box of brownie mix and decided to mix it up. Baking would give her something to do with her hands, and after the stress of the last few days, she could use the chocolate.

She had just slid the pan into the oven when Jack returned to the kitchen, hammer and nails in hand. "Where did you find those?" she asked.

"I found a toolbox in the ruins of the office. It wasn't too badly damaged in the fire." He hammered a nail into the windowsill, then pulled it out. "Come here, Ian—I want to show you something," he called.

Ian came running and Jack dragged a kitchen chair over to the window for the boy to stand on. "See how this nail is sticking up from the window-sill?" Jack asked.

Ian nodded.

"Right now the nail keeps anyone from opening the window from the outside," he said. "Now pull on the nail for me. You'll have to tug hard."

The boy grasped the nail with both hands and pulled. "I got it out!" he crowed, and held up the nail.

Jack took it from him and slid it back into the hole. "If you need to get out of the window—if there's a fire or your mom or I tell you to climb out the window—all you have to do is pull out the nail and push up on the sash. Can you remember that?"

Ian nodded. "Can we try now?"

Jack laughed. "I don't think so. I just wanted to make sure you knew what to do in an emergency." He handed the boy half a dozen nails. "Why don't we go find a chunk of wood and you can hammer these in for me."

"All right." The boy raced out of the room, clutch-ing the nails.

Andrea looked after him. "Are you sure hammer-ing nails is a good idea?" she asked. "He might smash his thumb."

"He might. But he'll be okay. It's good for their

hand-eye coordination. And kids love to hammer things. At least, I did." He started to leave the room but stopped when his phone buzzed. "Hello?"

She studied his face as he listened to the call. The faint lines on his forehead deepened. "I guess all we can do is wait," he said, then hung up.

He turned to Andrea. "That was my boss. He says the local plowing crews are focused on clearing major roads and areas where people are living. This area is low priority. It's going to be a while before they get to us."

She tried not to show her disappointment. She wanted to be in her own home, with clean clothes and internet access and a good cup of tea. But Jack couldn't do anything to bring her those things any faster, so why waste breath complaining. "I guess it's a good thing I made brownies," she said.

"Jack! You said you'd help me nail things!" Ian called.

"Go," she said. "I appreciate you keeping him occupied."

"All right. Call me if you need anything."

I'm beginning to feel as if I need you all the time, she thought, but it was too soon to say so. When she returned to her normal life, she might feel differently. She didn't know yet if Jack was someone she could depend on not just to protect her in times of danger, but to stick with her when things were a lot less exciting.

JACK FOUND SOME shorter lengths of firewood and arranged them on the floor in front of the woodstove. The brick hearth made a good place for Ian to try out his carpentry skills. Jack showed the boy how to hold the hammer and helped guide the first few swings. After Jack let go, Ian missed the nail more often than he hit it, but he seemed to be having a ball.

Jack sat back and puzzled over their mysterious visitor. Was it possible an animal—maybe the pack rat from cabin two—had come into the house and taken the oatmeal and milk? But what animal was large enough to carry off the saucepan and the can?

If Gravel Voice had been wearing a ballistics vest, it was possible he had survived the shot, but then Jack wouldn't have seen blood on the front of his shirt. And surely the boss would have left in the car with the rest of his men. Even if for some reason he had stayed behind, he would have focused on obtaining a weapon, not leftover breakfast. So that left someone else for the thief. A stranded camper? A felon on the run? He'd ask Blessing to check with local law enforcement for reports of other thefts in the area or recently escaped convicts or missing campers.

"I'm tired now." Ian laid aside the hammer and looked up at Jack.

"You did a good job." Jack admired the row of crooked nails. "Why don't you lie down on the sofa and rest up from your hard work."

"Okay." The boy crawled up onto the sofa.

Jack set aside the hammer and nails and went into the kitchen, where Andrea was just taking the brownies from the oven. "Smells good." He nuzzled the back of her neck. "The brownies, too."

She swatted him away, but her eyes shone. "Where's Ian?" she asked.

"He's on the sofa, taking a nap."

"He lay down without a fuss?"

"It was his idea. He said he was tired."

She switched off the oven. "That's not like him. I'd better go check on him."

She left the kitchen and Jack retrieved the backpack and spread the papers on the table once more. If he could figure out exactly where Center Line Gulch was located, he could relay the information to the team and they could go in and investigate. If it was another hideout, Anderson and his pal might have headed there, thinking they would be safe. The team might even get lucky and find the ringleader, Duane Braeswood, and wrap up this whole case.

Andrea returned to the kitchen. "He feels a little feverish," she said. "It might just be from all the excitement the past couple of days, but I'm worried he's coming down with something. I'll feel better when I can get him home."

"Do you want me to call my boss and tell him it's an emergency?" Jack asked.

"No. It's just a slight fever. He may feel better

after his nap." She sat across from him. "Have you figured out anything from those papers?"

"No luck with the Russian pamphlet." Jack tapped the booklet. "It doesn't have illustrations, only a lot of words and what look like mathematical formulas. How's your calculus?"

"Nonexistent," she said. "One of the reasons I was attracted to psychology was that it doesn't require a lot of math."

"I took plenty of math for my robotics courses, but none of this makes sense to me." He set aside the pamphlet. "The map is a mystery, too. Did whoever owned this backpack have the map to help him find this place, or is the circled area the most important information?"

"It must be marked for a reason," she said.

"It could be another hideout or a meeting place, the home of one of the group members, or even a place they planned to rob or carry out an act of sabotage." He continued to stare at the network of black-and-white squiggles and lines until they blurred, then let out a frustrated breath. "I'll have to let the team figure it out. If we compare it to full-size maps of the area, we should be able to find a match."

"It's frightening not knowing what they were up to," she said. "Do you really think Ian's kidnapping was just a way to get back at you, or did they have something else planned?"

"I wouldn't put anything past these people. They

don't hesitate to use or kill innocent people to further their agenda. The organization is like an octopus. Every time we cut off one arm, there's another arm wreaking havoc. It won't stop until we get to the leaders."

"Mama! Mo-om!" Ian's wail had them both on their feet and running toward the living room. They found the boy sitting up on the sofa, his hair mussed and his face flushed. Lip trembling, he held up his arms to his mother.

Andrea gathered him close. "Honey, what is it?" she asked, pushing his hair back from his forehead. "What happened? Did you have a bad dream?"

"The man. The man was here."

Andrea and Jack exchanged looks. "What man, honey?" she asked.

"The man at the window." Ian pointed to the window at the side of the house. "He was trying to get in." Ian buried his face against his mother's shoulder and began to sob.

Jack raced outside and leaped off the porch. He spotted no one at the side of the house or running away, but in the snow beneath the window were the fresh imprints of a man's shoes, distinct from the prints Jack had made when he had removed the plywood from the window earlier.

He scanned the area around the cabin. The footsteps faded out at the edge of the trees, where the ground was rougher and the snow less deep. Trees came to within a few feet of the building on two sides, but those at the back had been thinned, providing a clear view of the river. Sunlight glinted off the rushing current and a fish-cleaning station nearby. A snow-covered path led from where Jack stood to the water, but the snow showed no sign of tracks, and the riverbank provided no good hiding place for a man on the run.

To Jack's left, trees closed in. Though the dense underbrush would make movement difficult, someone standing only a few dozen yards away would be hidden from anyone in the camp. Jack started walking toward the river, then circled around and began moving, as quickly and quietly as possible, through the trees along the camp boundary.

A rabbit exploded from beneath a stand of scrub oak to Jack's left. Pistol drawn, he whirled toward the sound. Branches shook and a squirrel let out a furious chattering as something large and heavy moved away from Jack.

Jack plunged toward the movement. "FBI!" he shouted. "Stop, or I'll shoot." He ducked behind a large tree trunk, braced for a barrage of gunfire.

But only silence greeted his demand. The movement stopped, not a twig or tree branch moving. After a few seconds, the squirrel resumed fussing. Staying in the cover of tree trunks, Jack took one cautious step forward and then another. He couldn't see his quarry, but he knew he had to be close.

"P-please don't shoot me."

The voice wasn't what he expected. The words were quavery and high-pitched, more like the voice of a child than a grown man.

"I won't hurt you," Jack said. *Not if I don't have to.* "Put your hands up and move to where I can clearly see you."

The tall, slender figure stepped into the cleared space beneath a broad-trunked pine tree. Dirty-blond hair fell across a pale face, the cheeks fuzzed with a patchy, thin beard. The jeans and hoodie he wore were dirty and torn, and he had a blanket draped around his shoulders. Jack relaxed, though he held the gun steady on the boy. "What's your name?" he asked.

"Brian. Brian Keeslar. Who are you?"

Jack ignored the question. "What were you doing looking in the window of that cabin?" he asked.

"I was just trying to see if there was anybody in there."

"So you could break in again and steal something?"

"I just wanted food. I didn't want anything else. Please, mister. You're not going to shoot me, are you?" The boy began to cry—and Jack could see that he was a boy, though an almost grown one— shoulders shaking, tears flowing down his cheeks.

Jack lowered the gun slightly. "What are you doing here, kid?" he asked.

Brian sniffed. "It's a long story."

"Come on." Joe motioned toward the cabin. "Let's go back to the camp. You can get something to eat and tell me all about it."

Chapter Ten

"You promise you won't hurt me?" Brian asked.

Jack holstered the gun. "I won't hurt you," he said.

"Are you really with the FBI?"

"I really am."

The boy wiped his face with the back of his hand. "Maybe you can help me," he said.

"I probably can. Come on. Let's go inside." Jack took hold of the young man's arm, more to keep him from startling and running back into the woods than anything else. He looked scared half to death. Jack led him up onto the porch of the cabin and opened the front door. "Andrea, we've got a visitor," he called, and ushered Brian inside.

She was still holding Ian, rocking him in her arms. The boy turned his head to look at their visitor but said nothing. "Andrea, this is Brian," Jack said. "Brian, this is Andrea and Ian."

"Hello." Brian kept his eyes on the floor and shifted from foot to foot.

"Why don't we all go into the kitchen and sit

down," Jack said. "I'll fix Brian something to eat and he can tell us his story."

Andrea and Brian sat at the table, Ian in her lap. Jack opened a can of chili and heated it, then served it to Brian with crackers and a glass of water. At the last minute, he cut two brownies from the pan on the counter and put them on a napkin beside the bowl of chili.

"Thanks," Brian muttered. He stared at the food.

"Go ahead and eat," Andrea said. "We'll wait until you're done to talk."

The boy ate quickly, as if he was afraid someone would take the food from him. When he was done, he pushed the plate away. "That was the best meal I've had in a while," he said.

Jack took the chair across from him. "It looks like you've been living rough for some time," he said. "What's your story?"

The young man shifted in his chair. "First would you tell me what you're doing here?" He glanced at Andrea. "I mean, you seem like a nice family, but this is a funny place for a vacation."

Jack glanced at Andrea. Ian had fallen asleep, his head on her shoulder. "We're not on vacation," he said. "We're here because the men who were living here kidnapped Andrea's son. We were able to rescue him, but they got away. Snow has blocked the roads, so we're stuck here until the plows get out this far."

"Oh, man." Brian buried his face in his hands and

Jack thought he might start to cry again. After a few seconds, he looked up. "I can't believe they did that to a little kid. I wish you had shot them all."

"Did you know the men who were here?" Andrea asked.

"I guess you could say that." Brian made a face. "They weren't my friends, if that's what you think."

"What was your relationship to them?" Jack asked.

"They kidnapped me, too. About three months ago, as close as I can tell."

"Your poor parents," Andrea said. "They must be worried sick."

Brian rubbed his hands up and down his arms. "It's just my dad. I'm not sure he even knows I'm missing. Or still missing."

The kid was right. This was a complicated story. "Why don't you start at the beginning," Jack said.

"Yeah, okay." Brian stared off to the side for a long moment, saying nothing. Then he began.

"My dad is a physicist, Barry Keeslar. He does a lot of work with nuclear energy, enriching uranium, experimenting with fission and fusion and all that stuff. Right now he's in Russia, or maybe Iceland—it's hard to keep track of his schedule. He travels around consulting with different governments and stuff." He shrugged. "I'm not all that sure. I haven't seen him in like ten years and we only talk on the phone every few months. My parents divorced when

I was a little kid, but he never remarried or had any other kids or anything. My mom died last year and since then I've kind of been on my own."

Andrea reached out and covered his hand with her own. "I'm very sorry. That must have been hard."

He hesitated a moment before moving his hand away. "I did okay," he said. "I was going to school in Boulder. I'm a freshman at the University of Colorado. My dad paid for that, at least. I had friends and a job and everything. Life was good. Then one day I'm closing up the pizza place where I work weekends and these two guys dressed in black come in. I figure they want to rob the place. My boss already told me if that happened, I'm supposed to cooperate. Shut up and give them what they want. But what these guys wanted was me. They knocked me out and the next thing I know, I wake up here, tied up and chained to a bed."

"Who kidnapped you?" Jack asked. "Do you know their names?"

"There were three main guys. The one in charge they called Chief, but he slipped a couple of times and I think his real name was Jerry. I never heard last names. The older guy who stayed in this cabin with me was Leo, and they called the other guy Andy, though he acted like he hated the name. Which only made the other two use it more. There were other people in and out of here a lot, but most of them, I never knew their names."

"And they held you here for three months?" Andrea looked stricken at the thought.

"They told me as soon as my dad 'cooperated,' they would let me go." He made air quotes around the word *cooperated*. "I didn't think it was money they were after, though I guess my dad has plenty of that. It might have had something to do with his job, but they wouldn't answer any of my questions, and they didn't like it if I asked."

"What did your father do when they contacted him?" Andrea asked.

"I don't know what my father did. From what little I overheard, I think at first this bunch was having a hard time getting ahold of him. He moves around a lot and he's kind of the absentminded-professor type. He doesn't always answer his phone or check his email, especially when he's involved in a project."

"The police must have been looking for you," she said. "Your friends and professors must have noticed when you didn't show up for class."

"I don't think so. They grabbed me just before a three-day weekend, so my friends probably thought I left town. When I didn't come back, they probably thought I'd quit school or transferred somewhere else. It happens."

"So they kept you here for three months," Jack said.

"Yeah. They kept me tied up a lot of the time, but after a while they'd untie me and let me walk around.

They told me they'd kill me if I tried to get away and I believed them. They were mean. Sometimes they'd knock me around, not because they were angry or anything, just because they were bored. They fed me the same boring canned stuff they ate, but sometimes Leo would 'forget' to give me meals. The longer I stayed here, the more worried I got. I figured sooner or later they were going to kill me."

"How did you get away?" Jack asked.

"A couple of days ago, they left me alone. I couldn't believe it. I overheard them arguing and I guess Leo was pitching a fit about always having to stay here, guarding me, so they left me tied up and all drove away together. I couldn't believe it. I had a broken bottle I'd found in the trash a couple of weeks back. I'd stashed it under the mattress and as soon as they left, I got it out and used it to saw at the ropes. It took forever and I was terrified they would come back before I got done, but at last I was free. About that time they came back and I ran into the woods. I thought I would hike to the road and hitch a ride, but it started snowing and then I got lost in the woods. By the time I ended up at the road, the bridge was blocked, so I came back here, only to find they were gone and you folks were here."

"Why didn't you come to us for help?" Andrea asked.

"I thought you might be part of their group," he said. "They've had all kinds of people in and out of here while I've been here. Some of them stay for a single night, some for a couple of weeks."

"You thought I was a terrorist?" Andrea's face betrayed her horror at this idea.

"There was a woman here once, about your age," Brian said. "Leo said she was the daughter of someone important. They didn't keep her tied up or anything, but I got the impression she didn't want to be here. They kept me out of sight while she was here. After a couple of days she left."

"I hate to think of you out in the snow, cold and hungry," Andrea said. She stroked Ian's sleeping head. "You're safe now."

"We'll locate your father and contact him as soon as we're back in Durango," Jack said. "I'll want you to give a statement to the FBI and look through some pictures to try to identify the men who held you. When we find them, we'll ask you to testify against them."

"I'll do it." He sat up straighter. The meal, and maybe talking about his ordeal, had vanquished the hunted look.

"For now, can you tell me anything about what the people here were up to?" Jack asked. "Anything you overheard about other people or locations or anything like that could help."

Brian shook his head. "I can't think of anything right now. Mostly they just groused to each other about being stuck here while their bosses got to live in some fancy house somewhere."

"Did they mention the boss's name?" Jack asked.

"No. They just called him Boss. When they weren't grousing about him, they liked to shoot off guns in the woods, and sometimes Leo went fishing. Jerry went on sometimes about the importance of their mission and how they were saving America, but the other two seemed to be in it for the money. They talked about what they were going to buy when they got their big payoff, but I never did figure out where the money was supposed to come from."

"You may remember more later," Jack said. "Whatever you can tell us will be helpful. Even details you think are unimportant could help us fill in another piece of the puzzle."

"I'll do whatever I can to help you nail these guys," Brian said. He turned to Andrea. "Is your little boy okay now?"

"The kidnappers didn't hurt him, if that's what you mean." She laid her hand protectively on Ian's head. "But he's running a fever and not feeling well. I think the stress of all this has made him sick."

"Do you know when the snowplows will be here?" Brian asked. "I don't want to stay around here any longer than I have to. I'm worried Jerry and his friends might come back."

"Jerry—" Andrea began.

"Jerry won't be bothering you anymore." Jack

caught Andrea's eye and shook his head. No sense going into the whole story of Jerry and his shooting. There would be time enough for that once they had confirmed the man was dead. "I'll call my boss again and let him know we've found you and get an update on our rescuers."

He moved into the living room and took out his phone. The battery was getting low. As soon as he completed this call, he would have to dig out his charger.

"Blessing." As always, the special agent in charge barked the word like a command.

"Jack Prescott, sir. We've had a new development."

"What is it this time?"

"We've met up with a teenage boy who says Anderson and his group held him hostage for three months. He escaped right before they brought Ian McNeil here and has been hiding in the woods near the camp. His name is Brian Keeslar and he says his father is a nuclear physicist. He thinks the group was trying to force his dad into doing some work for them."

"Give me that name again?"

Jack gave him the boy's name and the name of his father. "Apparently, his dad is working overseas and hard to get ahold of. Brian doesn't know if the kidnappers succeeded in contacting him or not."

"If the kid spent three months with these people, maybe he can tell us more about them."

"That's what I'm hoping," Jack said. "It sounds like he had a pretty rough time of it, but he wants to cooperate. Any word on when we're getting out of here?"

"Not yet. I'll see what I can do to move you up the priority list, but apparently, there are a lot of people ahead of you."

"Tell them we've got a sick kid here. Ian is running a fever and not feeling well. I think—" A loud noise vibrating the air cut off Jack's words. He raised his eyes toward the ceiling and the noise overhead.

"Is that a helicopter?" Brian stood in the kitchen doorway, Andrea behind him with Ian in her arms.

Jack opened the front door and looked out. "Sir, you didn't just send a helicopter to get us, did you?"

"Do you really think I have the budget to scramble a helicopter in a nonemergency situation?" Blessing asked.

"Then I think this just became an emergency situation," Jack said. He peered at the helicopter that was just clearing the treetops, preparing to set down in the middle of the camp. "I think Anderson has returned. And from the looks of things, he's brought reinforcements."

Chapter Eleven

Andrea clutched Ian so tightly he began to whimper. "It's okay, honey," she said. She smoothed the hair back from his feverish forehead, her heart hammering in time with the throbbing helicopter rotor. "What do we do?" she asked Jack.

"We've got to get out of here," he said. He ran past her into the kitchen and retrieved his coat and the pack. He turned to Brian. "We're going to run out of here straight to my truck. It's the black Ford parked out front. Andrea and Ian go in first, then you and me."

Brian's Adam's apple bobbed in his throat as he swallowed. "Can we get away from them?" he asked.

"We will." Jack slung the pack onto his back and drew his Glock. "Andrea, when I give the word, you make a run for it."

She woke Ian and helped him put on his coat, then shrugged into her own and retrieved the blanket from the bedroom and handed it to Brian. "Wrap up in this," she instructed. "Since you don't have a coat." She grabbed the other blanket from the sofa and draped it over Ian. Her instinct was to hide her baby from the men in that helicopter. "I'm ready," she said.

"Wait until I give the word." Jack eased open the door and peered out. Almost immediately, gunfire exploded from the helicopter, bullets slamming into the wood at his feet and beside him. Andrea screamed as he dived back into the room. Brian shoved the door shut, then retreated toward the kitchen.

"We'll have to go out the back window," Jack said, and led the way into the kitchen. By the time Andrea joined him, he had already removed the nails he'd driven into the windowsill earlier and pulled a kitchen chair over to the counter. "Brian, you go first," he instructed. "You can help Andrea with Ian. Andrea, as soon as you're out, head for the river. I'll be right behind you."

Brian's face had lost all color and his hands trembled as he clutched at the windowsill. But he didn't hesitate to crawl through the opening. His feet hit the ground below with a soft *thud*. No gunfire followed him.

"Take this." Jack passed the pack through the window, then reached for Ian.

Andrea clutched at the boy, reluctant to let him go. But Ian held his arms out to Jack and cuddled against his neck. Jack smoothed his hand down the boy's back. "It's going to be okay, buddy," he murmured.

Brian took Ian and held him while Andrea crawled through the window. She landed crookedly and fell but was immediately on her feet and taking her son.

"Go!" Jack commanded. "Run to the river. I'll meet you there."

Brian reached for her hand, his grip stronger than she had expected. "Come on," he said. "We have to hurry before they figure out what we're doing."

The race for the river felt like running in a dream, time slowing as she slogged through the heavy, wet snow. She carried Ian cradled against her chest, the blanket draped over him. His weight dragged at her. Brian, no longer holding her hand, moved farther and farther ahead of her. Her breath came in pants, lungs straining, ears attuned for the sound of the gunfire she feared would mow her down.

Then she was standing behind the fish-cleaning shelter with Brian. When Jack joined them a minute later, she almost sobbed with relief. "I shoved the chair away and closed the window behind me," he said. "Maybe that will delay them figuring out how we got out."

He took the pack from Brian and put it on, then reached for Ian. She surrendered the boy without protest. Jack would protect him, she was certain.

"Where do we go now?" Brian asked.

"If we stay in the woods, they won't be able to

get a clear shot from overhead," Jack said. "We need to find a safe place to hide before they come after us on foot."

"I can't hear the helicopter anymore," Andrea said. Did that mean the kidnappers were already coming after them?

"They've probably landed," Jack said. "It will take them a few minutes to search the cabin and figure out we're not there. The faster we move, the more distance we can gain on them."

"I know a place we can hide," Brian said. "I spent the night there last night. It's an abandoned mine about a mile from here, maybe a little more. But we'll have to climb a pretty steep slope to get to it."

Jack clapped him on the back. "Let's go."

They jogged through the woods, maneuvering around downed trees and clots of underbrush too thick to push through. They stumbled through drifts and over hidden rocks, but beneath the sheltering trees the snow wasn't as deep. Jack broke trail and the others followed in his footsteps. No chance of hiding their path from anyone who might be searching behind them. Their best hope was to move as quickly as possible and find a good place to hide.

The scent of fresh pine and spruce washed over them, clean and bracing. Brian directed them west, the elevation gradually increasing.

Soon Andrea was out of breath. "I definitely have to get to the gym more often when this is over," she panted as she followed Jack and Brian up an ever-steeper slope. Jack stopped to wait for her. "How's your leg?" she asked when she caught up with him.

"It's okay." But his grimace of pain told her otherwise. He should be at home, resting and recovering, instead of climbing a steep slope with the burden of a child in his arms.

"Let me take Ian," she said.

"No. I've got him," he said.

"I want to stay with Jack," the boy said, as if he knew the man, even injured, was more capable of getting him safely up the slope than his mother.

They continued climbing, with Brian in the lead now, taking them to his hideout. "It's not much farther." Brian stopped and looked back over his shoulder to Jack. "Should we be doing something to cover our tracks?" he asked.

Jack shook his head. "There's no point in that now. They know we're out here. Our best bet is to find a good hiding place and lie low until we can get help. When we're settled in, I'll call my boss and give him our location. He'll get help to us."

Andrea didn't ask how that help was going to cross a blocked road and get past the kidnappers to reach them. This was the FBI, after all. Maybe they would call in the National Guard or send in a SWAT team. She'd settle for the cavalry on horseback if it meant she and her son would be safe.

"I have to pee," Ian announced.

"Hold on a little longer, buddy," Jack said. "We're going to stop soon."

"I have to pee now!" He pounded his fists against Jack's shoulders and squirmed in his arms. "Put me down."

Jack looked at Andrea. "Tell him to hold on just a little longer," he said. "We need to put more distance between us and Anderson's bunch before we stop."

She took Ian from him. "You can hold it a little longer, can't you?" she asked.

"No, Mama. I have to go." He tried to get down, his face screwed up as if at any moment he might start screaming.

"It will be easier if we stop and let him go now," Andrea said. "It won't take a minute." She lowered the boy to the ground. "Okay, honey, you can go now."

"Not with everyone watching," he protested.

"We'll just, um, turn our backs," Jack said. He turned around and motioned for Brian to do the same.

"Hurry, honey," Andrea said.

Jack didn't like letting Andrea and the boy out of his sight, but he hadn't heard any sounds of pursuit since they had left the camp, and Andrea wouldn't go far.

Her footsteps faded as she led Ian into the woods. He heard the soft tones of her voice as she reassured her son. The sound reassured Jack, too. As long as he could hear her, he knew she was all right.

"How much farther until we reach this mine?" he asked Brian.

"Maybe another twenty minutes." Brian wrinkled his forehead. "I kind of found it by accident, so I wasn't really keeping track of time."

"It is safe to go into?" Jack asked.

"I didn't go very far. But the entrance is pretty big and dry. It's just this cave carved out of rock. And you have a nice view of the valley from the entrance."

A good view of whatever was approaching them sounded safe to Jack. He turned around. "Andrea? Are you almost finished?"

No answer.

"Andrea!"

The sound of something moving very fast through the underbrush toward him had him resting a hand on his gun and looking for suitable cover. "Jack!" Ian's shout sent ice through Jack's veins. "The bad men took Mommy! She's gone!"

ANDREA FOUGHT BACK tears as a large man dressed all in black and armed with a semiautomatic rifle dragged her away from the others. She had let Ian run ahead of her as they made their way back toward the others, hoping that if he had a chance to stretch his legs now, he would be less restless later.

Her captor had stepped out from behind a tree,

clamped a hand over her mouth and wrapped her in an iron-hard grip before she could so much as squeak. He had slipped the gun from her waistband and pinned her to him almost before she realized what was happening. Ian had stopped and looked back. His eyes widened when he saw her.

Run! She'd wished she could scream this silent plea. He must have seen the message in her eyes, however, since he'd whirled and raced away.

Her captor, who seemed to be alone, dragged her back through the woods. No way did she have the strength to fight him, so she made herself go limp in his arms. At least he seemed to be moving away from the others, not toward them. If Ian could get to Jack, her boy would be safe.

Her captor dragged her, with seemingly little effort, at least a quarter mile, to where four other men waited by the river. All were similarly dressed in black, with masks over their faces and weapons slung on their shoulders. She tried to memorize details about them, but their uniforms had clearly been designed to hide any distinguishing features. She was pretty sure none of these men were Anderson. They all looked bigger and more menacing than the man who had snatched her purse.

"Look what I found." Her captor shoved her toward the others. She landed on her knees in the snow at their feet—four pairs of identical black boots ranged around her.

"Where are the others?" The shortest and slightest of the group spoke, his voice slightly nasal.

"They're up the trail a little ways, near where I found her." Her captor jerked his head in the direction they had come. "The little boy and the first kid—Keeslar's son—and the fed."

"If you got close enough to see them, why didn't you just take them out and save us the trouble?" another of the group said.

"Grabbing the woman was better," her captor said. "We'll use her as bait to get the other three without any risk to us."

The shorter man nudged her with the toe of his boot. She'd been too afraid to move from her position on the ground. "Can you talk?" he asked.

"I don't have anything to say to you."

The reply earned her a sharp kick. "You want to see your kid or that fed again, you'd better cooperate," he said.

Her captor grabbed her arm and dragged her to her feet.

"What do you want me to do?" she asked, trying to sound stronger than she felt. She had always believed bullies played on weakness.

His smile sent a chill through her. "First we're going to tie you up," he said. "Then we're going to make you scream."

IAN CLUNG TO JACK, tears streaming down his face, breath coming in hiccuping gasps. Jack knelt and tried to calm the boy, even as his own heart hammered in his chest. "Tell me exactly what happened," he said, his hand firm on the boy's shoulder. "Who took your mother? How many people were there?"

"J-just one man. A big man, dressed all in black—like a ninja!"

"He grabbed your mother, but you got away?" Jack asked.

"She let me run ahead and when I looked back to make sure she was coming, he was hugging her. He had a big gun and a mask on his face."

His bottom lip quivered and Jack patted his shoulder, trying to hold off the tears. "Were there any other people with the man?"

Ian sniffed. "No. It was just him. He started dragging Mama away." He pulled on Jack's arm. "We have to go find her."

"We will find her, buddy, I promise." He patted the boy's shoulder again and stood, pulling his phone from his pocket as he did so.

"Can you get someone here to help us?" Brian asked.

Jack shook his head. "No signal." He stowed the phone, already shifting his focus to strategizing to free Andrea. But first he had to see to his other obligations. "You have to promise me something, too," he said.

"What?" Ian asked.

"You have to promise to stay with Brian while I go and get your mom. Can you do that for me?"

Ian regarded the young man critically, then looked back at Jack. "I want to go with you," he said.

"I know you do. But I don't want these men to try to hurt you. Instead, I want you to go with Brian to a hiding place he knows."

"Yeah." Brian straightened his shoulders and did his best to look excited. "It's like a secret clubhouse I know about. I'll take you with me."

Ian still looked doubtful.

Jack bent to put his face close to Ian's. "It's really, really important to me that you go with Brian," he said. "I'm going to fight these bad guys and get your mother and then we'll come to the clubhouse where you and Brian will be waiting."

Ian stuck out his lower lip but nodded. "All right."

Jack straightened and pulled Brian aside. "I want you to take this." He slipped the pack off his back. "Have you ever shot a gun?

Brian's eyes widened. "No."

Jack unzipped the pack and took out the pistol. "I hope you don't have to use this, but the people who are after us are armed, and I don't want to leave you helpless." He showed Brian how to operate the safety. "The rules are simple—don't put your finger on the trigger until you're ready to shoot, don't ever point it at anything you don't want to shoot, and when you do shoot, be aware of what is around and behind your target. Don't use it if you don't have to."

"No, sir, I won't."

Jack replaced the gun in the pack and adjusted the straps to better fit Brian. "How do I find this mine where you're headed?" he asked.

"Keep climbing up this mountain and above tree line you'll see the opening to the mine," Brian said. "It's kind of a scramble to get there, but there's sort of a trail."

Jack slipped his cell phone from his pocket and handed it to the boy. "I'm hoping you'll be able to get a signal when you get above tree line," he said. "When you're able to call out, call the number for Ted Blessing and tell him what happened. He'll send help."

"What about you?"

"Andrea and I will meet you either at the mine or wherever the FBI takes you. Don't worry about us. You take care of Ian and yourself." He clapped the young man's shoulders. "You've survived a tough ordeal for three months—you can get through this."

"Yes, sir."

Jack squatted down in front of Ian. "Everything's going to be okay," he said. "Now, tell me—which way did the man take your mother?"

Ian pointed in the direction he had run from. Was the kidnapper taking Andrea toward the river? Or back to the camp? Jack straightened. "Okay, guys. You'd better get going. I'll see you both soon." He hoped.

When he was satisfied Brian and Ian were headed away from him, he began searching the ground in the area where he had last seen Andrea and Ian. The recent snow made it easier to track movements. He found where Ian's small tennis shoes had scuffed through the drifts and, a few yards later, spotted a portion of a man's large boot print and drag marks, as if from someone—Andrea?—being pulled backward across the ground.

He moved forward slowly, trying to stay in cover, following the boot prints and drag marks. He hadn't gone far when a woman's terrified scream shattered the woodland silence. Jack straightened and began running toward the sound.

Chapter Twelve

The screaming continued, a ragged, piercing note that made the hair on the back of Jack's neck stand on end. He slowed as he neared the sound, every sense attuned to his surroundings, alert for danger. A flash of blue caught his attention and he turned toward it, tensing when he spotted Andrea, tied to a tree, her head thrown back, mouth open in a keening cry that echoed in the otherwise still air.

He moved to within a few dozen yards of her, using the trunk of an old-growth juniper for cover. His first instinct was to rush forward and free her from whatever was making her scream that way, but he took a deep breath and forced himself to assess the situation rationally. No one else was around her, but he sensed whoever had tied her up this way was close, probably watching. She appeared unhurt. He couldn't see any blood or obvious injuries or even torn clothing. The screaming continued, but he realized it had a mechanical quality, like an amateur actor performing on cue. Had her captor ordered her to scream in order to draw him in?

Movement to her right caught his attention and he drew the Glock. But a man, wearing a mask and dressed in black, had already moved in beside Andrea and placed a knife to her throat. "You can come out now, Agent Prescott. I know you don't want to see this lovely lady bleed to death right in front of you."

Jack hesitated. The man in black brought the knife closer. Andrea cried out and a thin trickle of blood slid down her throat. Jack holstered the Glock and stepped into the clearing, his arms raised.

Four men, also masked and wearing black, moved out of the underbrush and surrounded him. One took the Glock and another bound his wrists behind his back. "Where is the backpack?" a shorter man with a nasal voice demanded.

"What backpack?"

The man slammed his fist into the side of Jack's head. His vision blurred and he struggled to remain upright. "What did you do with the pack you found in the cabin?" the man asked.

"I hid it."

"We're wasting our time with him." A different man spoke. "We should kill them both and go after the boy and the kid. They won't get far on their own."

"We need that pack," the short man said.

"He had it when I spotted them earlier." The man with the knife had moved away from Andrea and joined them. "He must have given it to the kid," he said.

"We'll go after the kids," the short man said. "But we won't kill them—yet. Tie him up with her."

Two of the men dragged Jack toward the tree. He resisted, earning another dizzying blow to the head. "Try that again and I will slit her throat," the first man growled, and shoved Jack hard against the same tree where Andrea was tied.

They bound Jack to the tree, his back to Andrea. Then four of them, including the man with the knife and the shorter man, left. One man stayed behind to guard the captives. He sat on a fallen log a short distance away, a rifle laid across his knees. "I'd love to have an excuse to shoot you, fed," he said. "So don't try anything."

The tips of Andrea's fingers brushed his. He curled his hands toward her, wishing he could reassure her. But the odds didn't appear to be in their favor. They would need a miracle to get out of this. Brian hadn't had time to reach tree line yet. Even if he had managed to call Agent Blessing right away, the team couldn't have mobilized quickly enough to get here, and they had no way of pinpointing Jack and Andrea's location.

"You shouldn't have come back for me," she whispered.

"You didn't really think I would abandon you, did you?"

"You should have stayed with Ian."

"Brian is with Ian. They'll be all right."

"Not with those four looking for them."

Jack studied their guard. He was heavier than the other men, though most of that bulk was probably muscle. He sat upright on the log, both hands on the rifle, his expression impossible to judge behind the black mask. "I'm not giving up yet," Jack said.

"You two stop blabbing over there," the guard ordered.

"What's with the ninja getup?" Jack asked.

The man grinned, revealing a crooked front tooth. "We heard you guys could identify us from surveillance videos and stuff, so the boss decided we should dress like this to maintain our anonymity."

"In your case, it didn't work, Gordon Phillips," Jack said. "Or should I just call you Gordo? That's what your prison buds called you, isn't it?"

The comment earned him a blow to the side of the head but it was worth it to see Gordo squirm. He loomed over them, having sprung from his seat on the fallen tree. "Who told you my name?" he demanded. "I never saw you before in my life."

"We know all about you and your pals," Jack said. Though Gordo—thanks to his crooked tooth—was the only man Jack had recognized.

"I ought to shoot you now," he said.

"Then your boss wouldn't have the chance to find

out what else I know," Jack said. "I'm guessing he wouldn't like that."

"I'd say you died trying to escape." Gordo hefted the rifle. "It happens."

"Then your boss would wonder why you weren't capable of looking after two tied-up prisoners on your own."

"Shut up!"

"Make me."

"Jack!" Andrea gasped.

Gordo took a step toward Jack. He raised the rifle butt-first over his head and Jack braced for the blow. But before Gordo could bring the weapon down on Jack's head, gunshots raked the clearing, bullets shredding bark from the tree where Jack and Andrea were tied and hitting the snow at Gordo's feet.

"What the—?" Gordo dived into the cover behind Jack and Andrea, but the bullets followed, the shots more focused on the man in black now. Gordo let out a scream and Andrea tensed.

The silence that followed rang in his ears. Jack tried to breathe normally, though his heart raced. "Gordo, are you okay?" he called.

Gordo swore. "I'm shot!"

"Come out with your hands up!" The voice that gave the order was strangely deep, with an echoing quality.

"Come in and get me!" Gordo shouted, and aimed a burst of gunfire toward the voice.

More gunfire peppered the bushes where Gordo

sheltered. Not a rifle, Jack decided, but a pistol, of a large enough caliber to be effective at close range.

Gordo returned the fire but shot wildly, unable to see his enemy.

Jack couldn't see anything, either. The shots continued, first from one side of the clearing, then the other. The shooter was close but obviously moving around. Another cry rose from Gordo. "All right," he cried. "Don't kill me."

"Throw out your weapon!" the voice ordered.

The rifle landed in the dirt a few feet from Jack.

"Your handgun, too," the voice ordered.

Muttering under his breath, Gordo tossed out not one but two handguns.

"Come out with your hands up."

"I'm wounded. I can't walk!"

"Then crawl."

The bushes swayed and bent as Gordo crawled from his cover. He had a black bandanna tied around his left thigh.

"Lay down with your face pressed to the ground," the voice ordered.

Gordo complied, his cheek nestled in the snow, arms stretched in front of him.

"Don't move or I'll kill you!" The voice was higher now—excited.

Gordo didn't move.

Silence followed, but Jack thought he detected movement through the bushes. After a tense moment, Brian, the pistol in one hand, a cone of paper in the other, stepped from the trees nearest Andrea. He stuffed the paper in his pocket and put a finger to his lips as he approached and knelt beside them. "I need something to cut you loose," he whispered.

"There's a knife in my pocket," Jack said.

Brian fished out the knife and freed Jack, then Andrea. "Where's Ian?" she asked. "Is Ian all right?"

"He's good," Brian said. "He's hiding somewhere safe."

Jack retrieved Gordo's discarded rifle and stood over the man. "Andrea, I need you to tie him up for me," he said.

Gordo had turned his head to watch them, but he hadn't moved. "You can't leave me here to bleed to death," he said.

Jack regarded the gunshot wounds to the man's thigh and forearm. "You're not going to bleed to death from those," he said. "Or would you rather I finished you off now?"

Gordo turned his head farther and glared at Brian. "You were the one shooting at me? You're just a kid."

Brian grinned. "Too bad I'm not a better shot, huh?" He gestured with the gun toward Gordo.

Jack gently took the gun from the young man. "Careful," he said, and slid the pistol into his pocket. Then he retrieved the two handguns Gordo had discarded.

Andrea finished knotting the rope around Gordo's ankles and stood. "I want to see Ian," she said.

"Take this." Jack handed her one of the guns. The other kidnappers probably had her handgun, along with his Glock. "Let's get out of here."

"This way," Brian said. He loped ahead of them, then stopped a few hundred yards down the river. He hooked two fingers in his mouth and let out a piercing whistle. "All clear!" he shouted.

"Look, Mama! I climbed a tree!"

Jack spotted Ian halfway up a leaning spruce. The boy scampered down the tree, climbing down the limbs as if he were climbing down a ladder. He ran to them and Andrea scooped him up in her arms. "I'm so glad to see you," she said.

"Brian and I came back to save you and Jack," Ian said.

Jack turned to Brian. "I told you to take Ian and keep yourselves safe," he said.

"I know what you told me, but I couldn't let you face those guys alone." Brian straightened his shoulders, as if bracing for a fight. "I knew there would be more than one of them. They always travel in packs. When they kidnapped me, there were four of them. Four of them against one teenager. I had to at least follow and make sure you were all right."

"And I'm glad you did." Jack clapped the young man on the back. "How many shots did you fire?"

"I don't know." He shrugged. "All of them. I used up all the ammunition, but I figured that guy back there didn't have to know that. It was pure luck that

I hit him. I wasn't aiming or anything. I just wanted to scare him off."

Jack decided not to point out that the young man's wild shooting had come close to injuring Jack and Andrea. What mattered most was that they were safe, at least for now.

"Jack." Andrea moved closer to him, Ian on her hip. "Hadn't we better get out of here? The others might come back."

Jack nodded. "When you were headed back here, did you see the other four men who were here?" he asked Brian.

"We saw them. But they didn't see us. We climbed the tree." He pointed to the spruce that had sheltered Ian. "They never even thought to look up. That's why I thought it would be a safe place to leave Ian while I tried to help you two."

"Good job. But Andrea's right. We need to get moving. If we don't reach help or a good hiding place before nightfall, we could be in real trouble."

Chapter Thirteen

The climb became much steeper, so that they had to grab on to branches to pull themselves up the outcroppings of rock. The sun had melted the snow in places, but in others the ground was still hidden beneath foot-deep drifts. Soon they were all wet to the knees, breathing hard from the exertion. Eventually, the cover of trees gave way to snow-pocked rock, yellow mine waste spilling down the slope in places. Andrea tried to focus on carefully placing her feet and hands as she climbed, shaken by how close she had come to death. She hadn't wanted to scream— hadn't wanted to lure Jack into her captors' trap, but when the one with the knife had threatened to cut her throat, she had given in, ashamed of her cowardice yet wanting desperately to live.

She would need more time to sort out her tangled emotions about everything that had happened. For now, they weren't out of danger yet. She tried not to think of how exposed they were on this bare slope, though tension pulled at her shoulders as she braced for gunfire that never came.

"Not much farther now," Brian said. "You can see the entrance from here." He stopped and pointed up. Following his line of sight, she spotted the patch of black against the pale rock.

"How do we get up there?" she asked.

"There's a path. I can just make it out." Jack looked back at them. He had reclaimed the pack and his phone from Brian and taken Ian as well, the boy clinging to his neck. Andrea marveled at how well her son had weathered the ordeal so far—thanks in no small part to Jack's calm courage, which strengthened them all.

"Just a little farther." Brian turned to pull her up beside him. In the space of a few hours, the young man had transformed from trembling waif to almost-brash teen, brandishing the pistol and vaulting up the mountain slope. Andrea suspected Jack's example—and Jack's trust in him—had restored the young man's weakened confidence. She didn't think this quality to inspire others was something the FBI had trained him to do. It was part of Jack's nature, like his crooked smile and the gentle way he touched her.

"Here we are." Above her, Jack stopped on a narrow rock ledge. He reached down to pull her up alongside him. Instinctively, she moved to one side, into the shadows cast by the mountain that rose behind them.

"Here you go, buddy." Jack set Ian on the rock shelf.

The boy stood on his own, gaping at the scenery. "Wow. We're really high up," he said.

"Come over here, honey." Andrea beckoned him to her side. "How are you feeling?"

"Okay." He looked up at her. "Can we go home now?"

"Soon, honey." She hoped it was very soon. She needed to feel safe again and to feel in control once more.

"Is it safe?" Jack asked Brian as he joined them on the ledge.

"Like I said, I didn't go very far in," Brian said. "I didn't have a light and it was really dark. But I spent the night just inside the entrance. It's not that comfortable, but I was out of the snow and wind and hidden."

"Let's see what we've got." Jack pulled a flashlight from a side pocket of the pack and switched it on. The rest of them followed him inside.

The entrance to the mine wasn't as creepy as Andrea had feared. The space, approximately eight feet deep and six feet wide, was cut into the rock and was dry and appeared bug- and varmint-free. The only smell was that of dust and the dried leaves that littered the floor. A tunnel, shored up with square timbers, led farther into the mountain.

"You can use this to sit on." Jack handed Andrea

the blanket and took off the pack. "I'm going to explore a little farther into the mine."

"I'll go with you," Brian said.

Andrea spread the blanket and settled down onto it. "I want to go with Jack," Ian said, and started after the men.

"You have to stay here with me," Andrea said.

"But I want to go with Jack." Ian stuck out his lower lip and his face clouded, the precursor to a storm.

"Do you want Mommy to have to stay here by myself?" She gently took his arm. "Jack and Brian will be right back. Stay here and I'll tell you a story."

"I don't want a story." But he let her pull him down into her lap.

"This is a good story," she said, wrapping her arms around him, as much to reassure herself as to keep him warm. "It's about a brave little boy. He was an explorer."

"What did he explore?"

She looked around her, searching for inspiration. "He climbed mountains," she said. "And he explored caves."

"Did he find treasure?"

"Yes, he found treasure. Gold and jewels."

"And a spaceship," Ian said. "He found a spaceship and he flew it to the moon."

She smiled. "What did the spaceship look like?" she asked.

"Andrea! Come here!"

Jack's voice was urgent enough that she was on her feet immediately. "What is it?" she called. "What's wrong?"

"You've got to see what we've found," he said. "Evidence that could blow this case wide-open."

JACK STARED AT the contents of the metal trunk he'd discovered in an alcove just off the mine tunnel. Neat putty-colored bricks, each individually wrapped in plastic, almost filled the container. The trunk's stainless outer surface, covered with only a light coating of dust, stood out from the old tools and piles of rock around it. Though a padlock dangled from the trunk's hasp, it had been undone and Jack had no trouble lifting the top to reveal this treasure trove.

"What is it?" Brian asked. "Drugs or something?"

Jack lifted out one of the bricks and hefted it in his hand. "I'm pretty sure it's plastic explosives," he said. "Probably C-4."

Brian took a step back. "It's not going to blow up, is it?"

Jack tossed the brick back into the trunk. "No danger of that. It needs a detonator to explode." He moved aside another brick to reveal a small cardboard box filled with a row of white plastic tubes attached to insulated wire cords.

Andrea joined them, out of breath from her race

down the tunnel with Ian. "What is it?" she asked. "What did you find?"

"Explosives," Brian said. "Lots of them."

Jack motioned to the trunk. "Plastic explosives. Probably stolen. I think it's the same stuff used in bombs set off at professional bicycle races around the country this past year. We caught a guy we think is connected to this group trying to sabotage the Colorado Pro Cycling Challenge in Denver in August."

"I remember hearing about that." Andrea shifted Ian to her hip and stared at the open trunk. "What's it doing here?"

"Good question." Jack closed the trunk. "It's not the sort of thing they use in mining."

"This place doesn't look like anyone has mined it in a hundred years." Brian picked up one of the chunks of rock piled beside the trunk. "What do you think these are? Geodes or something?" He examined the fist-sized specimen.

"Ore samples, maybe?" Jack shook his head. "They were probably here before the trunk was even brought in."

Andrea set Ian down and he immediately headed for the rocks and began picking them up. She glanced at the explosives. "I'm guessing that's enough to do a lot of damage," she said.

"That trunk is probably enough to level this mountain," he said. "At least, it would make a good-sized crater."

"Do you think Anderson and his bunch hid the trunk here?" she asked.

"We'll try to get fingerprints and DNA evidence off the trunk to be sure," Jack said. "But that would be my guess."

"I'm glad I'm not the one who had to haul that heavy trunk all the way up here," Brian said.

"They probably thought it was worth the effort because no one would ever find it up here," Jack said. "Before you found the place, probably no one had been here for decades."

"So this will help you connect Andy and the others to your Denver terrorists?" Brian asked.

"Yes. And it might even lead us to their ringleader— the man we've been trying to stop for the past year," Jack said. "He looks to be the money and the brains behind the operation."

"Somebody left their backpack," Ian said.

Jack whirled around and found the boy tugging at a black-and-orange backpack that had been covered by the pile of rocks. He knelt beside the boy and joined him in pulling the pack free. "Let's see what you've got there," he said.

"Maybe it will have a name or something," Brian said. "But I guess that would be too easy, huh?"

Jack hooked the end of his pocketknife into the ring attached to the zipper pull of the pack's main compartment and eased it open. He knelt and carefully upended the contents on the floor.

"No weapons in this one," Andrea observed.

"Candy!" Ian reached for the chocolate bar on top of the pile.

Andrea grabbed his hand and pulled him back. "You can't eat the evidence, dear," she said.

Jack slipped the candy back into the pack and fished out a man's wallet with the tips of his fingers. He flipped it open and stared at the driver's license, a cold chill sweeping over him.

"Mark Renfro." Andrea read the name over his shoulder. "He doesn't look like one of the men we saw at the camp."

"He's not." Jack closed the billfold and returned it to the pack, then stuffed everything else back inside.

"Who is he?" Brian asked.

"He's the brother of one of the agents in my unit. He disappeared on a hiking trip in Colorado over a year ago."

"Another kidnapping victim?" Andrea asked.

"Either that or a murder victim." He raised his eyes to meet hers. "We have to find these people and stop them."

"Yeah," Brian said. "As long as they don't find us first."

ANDREA SHIVERED AT Brian's reminder that they were far from out of danger yet. "What else is in the pack?" she asked. She didn't know what she was hoping for—something that could help them and get them out of this mess safely.

"Just clothing, some freeze-dried food and a first-aid kit," Jack said. "The kinds of things you would expect someone to take on a day hike in the mountains, which is what Mark was doing when he disappeared."

"Why would these guys want to kidnap him?" Brian asked. "Because they wanted to get back at his brother, the FBI agent?"

"I don't think so." Jack finished zipping up the pack and stood. "Like your dad, Mark Renfro is a nuclear physicist. The terrorists may want him to work for them."

Andrea wasn't willing to accept the conclusion her mind had leaped to. "Jack, you don't think these people are trying to build a nuclear bomb, do you?"

"I don't know what to think." He raked his hand through his hair. Like the rest of them, he was gray faced and weary, but anger sparked his words. "Judging by what they've done so far—the people they've killed and the lives they've disrupted—they'll stop at nothing to reach their twisted goals." He handed the pack to Brian. "This is important evidence," he said. "Can I trust you to keep it safe until I can turn it over to my team?"

Brian nodded and solemnly accepted the pack. "How are we going to get to your team from here?" he asked.

Brian took out his phone and studied the screen. "I'm not getting a signal in this tunnel. I may have to go outside. But I'll call my team leader and give him my coordinates. He can contact the people who can get us out of here and close in on this area and the camp while the others are still here."

"I don't like knowing those four are still out there looking for us," Andrea said.

"All we have to do is stay hidden until help arrives," Jack said. "Come on. Let's get back to the front entrance and I'll make the call."

He ushered them to the mine's entrance. "I'm bored," Ian announced.

"So am I." Brian sat cross-legged on the floor a few feet away from Andrea and Ian and began gathering pebbles. He used one of the pebbles to draw a circle in the dirt of the floor.

"What are you doing?" Ian asked.

"I'm going to have a battle with these rocks." He completed his circle, then put more rocks in the center of the circle. "See, I use this rock—" he chose a large roundish pebble "—to shoot the other rocks out of the circle." He demonstrated by flicking his thumb and forefinger against the pebble, sending it crashing into another rock, which shot out of the circle.

Ian inched closer. "Can I play?"

"Sure. It's better with two people anyway." He looked through the pile of pebbles and chose one for Ian to use as a shooter.

When Jack stepped out of the mine, Brian was showing Ian how to flick his thumb and forefinger in order to send his pebble crashing into others in the circle.

As he had hoped, his phone signal outside the cave was stronger. He called Ted Blessing's number and listened to it ring.

And ring. And ring. After five rings a mechanical voice informed him that he should leave a message. "This is Jack. We're in an abandoned mine about four miles east of the camp. Anderson and his group returned in a helicopter with reinforcements and—"

A long beep sounded, and then the phone went silent. Jack stared at the screen and pressed the button on the side of the phone to power it up again, but nothing happened. He swore under his breath and stared down at the woods below. In another hour or so the sun would set. If they were lucky, darkness would shut down the terrorists' search for them until the morning, but the prospect of a cold night without food or water wasn't one he looked forward to. He needed to find a way to get Andrea and Ian and Brian to safety, along with the evidence he had gathered. The sooner the team zeroed in on the camp and this mine, the sooner they could bring Duane Braeswood and his group to justice.

Andrea looked up when Jack stepped back into the mine. She had switched on his flashlight and arranged it in the center of the mine entrance, propped up with rocks, like a little candle sending its feeble glow on their gathered faces. "Did you talk to your boss?" she asked. "Is he sending someone to get us?"

"He didn't answer my call," Jack said. "I left a message with our location. Then the phone died." He looked away, not wanting to see the disappointment in her eyes. He should have charged the phone first thing this morning, when he saw the battery was low. His carelessness had put all their lives in jeopardy.

"Jack, come sit beside me."

Her voice was gentle, with no hint of judgment or reprimand. She patted the blanket beside her and he eased down next to her, trying to ignore the throbbing in his leg.

"This isn't your fault, you know," she said, with the same matter-of-fact tone he imagined she used when she talked to her patients.

"How did you know what I was thinking?"

Her smile—the fact that she could smile at all, considering the circumstances, and that she would smile at him—knocked him a little unsteady, as if the ground had shifted beneath his feet. "None of us would probably be alive right now without your help," she said.

"I'm betting you'd be alive," he said. "You're pretty resourceful and fearless."

"Not fearless. But it helps that I'm not just fighting for myself. Alone, I might give up, but I'll do anything to protect my son."

He followed her gaze to Ian, who was bent over the dirt circle, tongue protruding slightly as he concentrated on aiming his makeshift marble. "How is he doing?" Jack asked.

"He still has a fever, but he's not getting worse. We'll see what happens after nightfall."

Jack leaned his head back against the rough rock wall. "So you realize we'll probably have to spend the night here."

"Better to stay put than go stumbling through the woods at night." She nudged him. "You aren't really thinking you have to keep that chocolate bar as evidence, are you? I'll give you the wrapper, but that chocolate is going to be eaten if we stay here, along with that granola bar, and if you can figure out a way to get water and heat it, we'll eat that freeze-dried stew, too."

"If I was alone, I'd probably resist the urge to destroy potential evidence," he said.

"You're with a teenaged boy and a five-year-old—the very definition of eating machines," she said. "I don't care to listen to either one of them whine about being hungry if I can help it."

"What about you—aren't you hungry, too?" he asked.

"If I could get away with it, I'd claim that whole chocolate bar for myself."

Jack squeezed her hand, then glanced at Brian. "Brian doesn't strike me as much of a whiner."

"He's incredible. And what he's been through gives me nightmares. I want to wrap him up and feed him homemade cookies and then I want to find his lousy excuse for a father and box his ears and tell him exactly what I think of him."

"I love it when you're fierce." He kissed her cheek.

She closed her eyes. "Sometimes it's what keeps me going."

"I want to wrap you up in blankets and feed you cookies," he whispered. "I want to take care of you, the way you take care of others."

She opened her eyes and the soft look in them made him set aside, if only for a moment, the pain in his leg, worries about the men who were hunting them and the urgency of stopping a group of terrorists bent on destroying the country.

"This whole ordeal has given me a new perspective on the work you do," she said.

"What do you mean?"

"I don't think I realized before what a real threat the people you go after are. I mean, I knew it in the abstract, but now I've seen up close how ruthless and, well, evil, they are." She squeezed his hand. "What you and other men and women like you do is really important. I hate to think what the world would be like if people like Gordo and Anderson and the others were allowed to carry out their plans unchecked."

"Don't make me out to be some kind of hero," he

said. "I have to live in this world, too. A lot of what I do is about self-preservation."

"You can pretend that, but I know different. Nothing you've done the last few days has been selfish. You didn't have to go to that fishing camp to rescue Ian, and you didn't have to come looking for me when those men grabbed me. You walked right in to what you had to know was a trap. You did it because you put our safety above your own."

"You and Ian are important to me. I thought you knew that by now."

She ducked her head, so that he could no longer read the expression in her eyes. "What I'm trying to say is that everything that has happened makes me realize I've been looking at some things wrong. With Preston—I used to think he chose his job over time with family because the work was so macho and exciting. He enjoyed the rush more than he enjoyed nights at home reading bedtime stories or talking to me."

"The job can be macho and exciting, and anyone who tells you they don't enjoy the rush is lying." Jack slid his hand up to caress her shoulder. "But none of that is more important to me than the world away from work. That everyday life, with the people I love, is the real world. The one that really matters. The one I'm working to protect."

"I guess it really is all a matter of perspective," she said.

"I didn't know your husband, or the kind of man he was." Jack chose his words carefully, aware that he was treading on sensitive ground where maybe he had no right to trespass. "But he loved you enough to marry you, and he gave you a great son. If he lost sight of his priorities sometimes—it can happen to the best of us."

She nodded. "I know. I forgot about what is really important, too. You've helped me remember that."

He wanted to ask her what he had done to change her thinking. Was she trying to tell him that his being a law enforcement officer wasn't such a black mark against him anymore? That she could see a future with the two of them together? But now, when they were still in so much danger, didn't seem the right time to press her.

"Mom, I'm hungry." Ian made Jack's decision for him by crawling into his mother's lap and giving her a mournful look.

"I'm sorry we don't have any dinner to give you." She rubbed his back.

"Jack has chocolate and he's not sharing."

Three pairs of eyes regarded Jack—two of them accusing, one sympathetic and maybe a bit amused. "All right, all right." He held up his hands. "We'll eat whatever is in that pack. But you have to let me unwrap everything so I can at least try to preserve the wrappers in case there are fingerprints."

"Great!" Brian shoved the pack over to Jack. "I'm starving."

Using his pocketknife and two fingers, Jack opened the pack and eased out the chocolate bar and two granola bars. He slit the wrapper from each, shook the contents into his lap, then passed them to Andrea. "You divide everything up," he said.

She broke each granola bar in half and distributed the pieces. "Give mine to the boys," Jack said.

She started to argue, but apparently, the look in his eyes or the set of his jaw made her think otherwise. "All right."

Brian accepted a chunk of granola bar and sat back. "You know what's funny?" he said.

"What?" Jack asked.

"There aren't any maps in there." He nodded to the pack. "You'd think a guy going hiking in the mountains would at least have at trail map."

"Maybe he knew the trail really well," Andrea said. She broke off another section of granola bar and handed it to Ian.

"That's not it," Jack said. "The man who owned this pack, Mark Renfro, had a photographic memory. He had probably memorized the map."

"Seriously?" Brian asked. "I thought that kind of stuff was only in movies."

"Jack remembers faces like that," Andrea said. "He truly never does forget a face."

"That would come in handy picking people out of a police lineup," Brian said.

"That it does," Jack said. If only he could remember the man who had murdered Gus. Pain pinched his heart at the thought, but it wasn't as sharp as before. He hadn't thought of his friend, or his own failure to remember the killer's face, in a few days. Was it because he had been preoccupied or, as Andrea had suggested, was he learning to live with that blank spot in his head?

"I guess you're pretty sure this is Mr. Renfro's pack," Brian said. "Since his wallet is in there. Too bad he didn't stash his phone in there, too."

"The phone would be dead after all this time," Andrea said.

"Not if he shut it off." Brian shrugged. "I guess we couldn't get that lucky, huh?"

"I don't know," Jack said, studying the pack. Back there in the mine tunnel, he had given the contents only a superficial look, reasoning he could examine it more thoroughly when he had it back at team headquarters. But now he noticed zipped pockets on the sides that he hadn't bothered to open before. He reached for the zipper on one of them now.

The cell phone was an older, no-frills model, not even a smartphone. But that meant no apps or Wi-Fi or Bluetooth to drain the battery as quickly.

"I don't believe it!" Brian whooped. "You found a phone."

Jack flipped open the phone. The screen was black. But when he pressed the on button, it glowed with life.

"Quick, call for help before it dies," Andrea urged.

Jack was already up and heading for the mine entrance.

Chapter Fourteen

Outside, dusk had descended and the first stars were visible in the clear sky overhead. Jack punched in the number for Ted Blessing. He groaned as it rang three times, then four. On the fifth ring, Blessing's clipped voice asked, "Who is this?"

"Jack Prescott."

"What are you doing calling on Mark Renfro's phone?"

"It's a long story. Did you get my message about our situation?"

"Yes, and we're trying to get someone in there to help you, but the only road in there is still blocked and we haven't gotten approval to hire a helicopter yet. Is Renfro there with you?"

"No. We found a backpack we think is his. At least, his wallet and ID and his phone were in the pack. We also found a box of plastic explosives we think Anderson and his bunch have stashed in the old mine where we're hiding. There may be more.

We need to get a team up here to go over this place. This could link Anderson's bunch to Braeswood."

"What's your situation now?"

"The four of us are getting ready to spend the night in this abandoned mine. We had an altercation this afternoon with five men—not Anderson, but a man who is in our database, Gordon Phillips, and four others. They were wearing masks, so I couldn't see their faces to identify them, but Gordo's bad dental work gave him away."

"What kind of altercation?"

Jack gave a brief summary of the afternoon's events, glossing over Brian's wild shooting. "We left Gordo tied up by the river, but the other four are still out here, searching for us. They're bound to remember this mine sooner or later. I don't think it will be safe to stay here in the morning."

"Are you in a position to hold them off?"

Jack made a quick assessment—they had the two handguns he had taken from Gordo, plus Gordo's rifle, but extra ammunition for only one of the weapons, a pistol that used the same ammunition as Jack's Glock. The handgun Brian had fired had no more bullets. They had no more food or extra clothing, and their only source of water was melted snow. "We've got three weapons and a limited amount of ammunition. They have high-powered rifles, a helicopter and more men. We can hold them off a little while from our position, but we can't move farther back into the mine. We do that and they could easily close off the entrance and trap us."

"Is there another way out of the mine?" Blessing asked.

"I don't know and it's not safe to look. From what I could see of the mine tunnel past the point where we found the explosives and Renfro's pack, some of the timbers have fallen and there's a lot of rubble. My judgment is that the whole structure is very unstable."

"All right. Sit tight as long as you can and we'll find some way to get to you. The local authorities must know that area. Maybe they can help. Are there any landmarks or distinguishing geographic features they can use to find you?"

Jack studied the area around the mine, but the sun had set and the few exposed rocks looked like black smudges against a gray background. He tried to recall any features he had noticed on the way up. "It's a mine, so there's quite a bit of waste rock around the entrance—red and yellow rock that stands out where the snow has melted because it's a different color from the other soil."

"Anything else?" Blessing asked.

Jack peered down the slope and his gaze locked on a pinpoint of light. It was joined by three other lights, each bobbing gently, gradually moving toward him. Fear, sharp and hard as a bayonet, lanced through him as he realized what he was looking at, but he forced the emotion away. "You're sure there isn't a rescue team already out looking for us?" he asked.

"I spoke to Search and Rescue less than half an hour ago and they said it would be tomorrow morning before they could get anyone to that area. They've been swamped."

Jack nodded, even though he knew Blessing couldn't see him. "Then we're in a lot more trouble than I thought," he said. "I'm pretty sure the four men we met up with earlier are headed this way."

"You can see them?"

"I can see their headlamps. They're maybe a mile away but climbing fast."

"How did they find you?"

He studied the tight formation of lights moving up the slope. The steady, organized way they moved hinted at a disciplined, determined group. "Do you remember the men Braeswood had with him in the Weminuche Wilderness—the ones who were hunting Travis Steadman and Leah Carlisle?" Though Jack had been in the hospital by then, he had read the team's official report later.

"Yes. But we captured them all."

"But you remember the type of men they were— ex-military and mercenaries, trained trackers."

"Yes."

"I think these are the same type of men. Braeswood isn't trusting ordinary babysitters with this one. These guys probably have night-vision goggles and scoped weapons."

"Try to hold them off until I can get help to you."

"Yeah. I've got to go now."

Not waiting for a response, he ended the call and took a last look at the lights below. They were strung out in single file now, having reached a narrower, steeper section of trail. At the rate they were traveling, he estimated they would be here in fifteen minutes or less.

ANDREA SANG SOFTLY to Ian, running through every lullaby she could remember in an effort to both soothe him and take her mind off their situation. Ian rested with his head against her chest, either sleeping or merely being quiet. She cupped her hand over his forehead. It felt hot.

Jack rejoined them and she looked up, her spirits lifting with his presence. Having him to lean on made all of this bearable. After she'd been alone for so long, it felt good to have someone to stand beside her in times of trouble.

"We've got to leave," he said. He zipped up Renfro's pack and handed it to Brian, then opened the other pack and removed the smaller of the two handguns he had taken from Gordo. "Take this," he said, thrusting it at Andrea. "Use it if you have to."

Andrea eased Ian to the floor and stood. His grim expression sent a chill through her. "What's going on?" she asked. "Did you reach your boss on the phone? What did he say?"

"There are lights headed this way. Probably men coming for us." He thrust the gun at her again. "Take this."

She did as he asked, the weapon heavy and cold as she slid it into her waistband at the small of her back. The kidnappers had taken the weapon Jack had given her earlier. She hoped the same thing didn't happen again.

"Maybe it's a search party looking for us." Brian had risen also, though the pack still sat on the ground. "I mean, if they have lights and everything, they're not trying to hide."

"They're not trying to hide because they know we're trapped." He suspected the lights were also intended to intimidate, to let them know what was coming and paralyze them with fear. But he wasn't going to sit here and not act. "Put the pack on and get ready to leave." Jack looked to Andrea. "Can you carry Ian? I need both my hands free."

In answer, she wrapped Ian in the blanket, then picked him up. "What did your boss say?"

"He can't get to us before these men do," Jack said.

"We outsmarted them once. We can do it again," Brian said. "They're bullies when there are more of them, but they're not smart or even particularly strong."

"These aren't Andy and Leo, or even Gordo by

himself," Jack said. "These are trained hunters. Former soldiers. Mercenaries. They've probably got high-powered weapons. They've done this kind of thing before."

"How do you know?" Andrea asked.

"Because that's how these people operate. I've seen it before." He checked the load on the larger of the two confiscated pistols, which took the same .44-caliber bullet as his Glock. "We've only got a few minutes," he said. He plucked the flashlight from the floor and switched it off, plunging them into darkness. Ian began to whimper and he heard the rustle of fabric as Andrea shifted to comfort the boy.

"What are we going to do?" Brian asked. His voice shook. "How are we going to get away from them?"

"We've got to climb, up and around the side of the mountain until we're out of sight. Then we have to head back down before they realize what's happening." He couldn't see their faces in the darkness, but he could feel their fear, like a cloud surrounding them. The plan wasn't a good one. If the men below had infrared goggles, they might be able to track their movements or figure out what they were doing. If they had thermal-imaging scopes or goggles, they would be able to track them, even in pitch blackness. Climbing in the darkness, they could fall or be injured. But staying put only to be trapped and shot like rats in a bucket wasn't an option. "Come on." He reached out and found Andrea's hand. "Let's go."

While miners and others had worn a path to the mine over the years, the only trail leading up had probably been made by deer or mountain sheep. A quarter moon cast a silvery glow over the snow, allowing Jack to pick out the narrow line of the path that led almost straight up from the mine entrance. "Brian, you go first," he instructed. "Crawl if you feel more stable. Move as quickly as you can, but take the time to feel for good hand- and footholds. Andrea will be right behind you with Ian, and I'll bring up the rear."

Andrea clutched at his arm. "Do you really think this is better than staying and fighting?" she asked. "Or surrendering to them."

"Surrendering isn't an option," he said. "I don't think they're going to waste any more time holding us hostage."

She let out a small cry as his meaning sank in.

"Mom, you're squeezing me," Ian protested.

"I'm sorry, honey. Put your arms around my neck, okay? And your legs around my waist. Now hang on tight. When we get to the top, I'll let you off for a minute."

She squeezed Jack's hand, then began climbing up the rock in front of him.

He checked below them. Their pursuers were moving more slowly now as they reached the steepest section, but they were making steady progress. If only he had a better weapon than a pistol and a rifle with only one magazine, he could try to mow them down. As it was, he might take out one or two of them, but the others would figure out where he was about the time he ran out of ammunition. If the waste rock were bigger, he could have shoved boulders down onto them, maybe started an avalanche.

The image of boulders careening down into the men below sparked an idea. *There's enough explosives here to level this mountain.*

He ordered the others to go ahead, then ran back into the mine, pausing only to switch on his flashlight once he was in the tunnel. Thirty seconds later, he stood in front of the box of explosives. His hands shook as he tore open the cardboard box of detonators and he forced them to steady. *Focus. Remember your training.*

He'd had a crash course in explosives at Quantico, primarily in order to familiarize himself with those used by terrorists, from suicide bombs to infrastructure sabotage. But part of the training had involved learning how to build a bomb of his own. He switched off the flashlight and willed that training to come back to him as he carried the detonator and the brick of C-4 to the mine entrance.

Their pursuers were close enough now that he could hear their movements—boots scraping on rock, the soft percussion of a dislodged pebble bouncing from rock to rock as it descended. He moved to the side of the mine entrance, to the shelter of a boulder, and forced his own breathing to become quiet and deep. In the dim moonlight, he carefully unwrapped the brick of explosives and molded the puttylike material around the detonator. He used only half of the brick, wary of taking out too much of the mountain and endangering himself and the others. He wanted to cause damage close to the kidnappers, but the destruction needed to be limited.

He forced himself to wait as long as possible. He wanted Andrea and the others to be as far from the mine entrance as possible when his homemade bomb went off. But he needed enough time to make his own getaway before the explosion.

He could make out faces beneath the headlamps the hunters wore—nothing recognizable, but the suggestion of chins and noses and human forms. They had removed their masks, probably to avoid hindering their peripheral vision. Their figures were bulky and dark, suggesting they wore packs and probably ballistics vests. The silhouettes of rifle barrels protruded from a couple of the packs.

When he judged that they were almost within firing distance from him, he took out the lighter and lit the end of the detonator cord. Then he stood and lobbed his makeshift bomb into the midst of the climbers.

Shards of rock exploded around him as bullets slammed into them. Jack scrambled up the slope, grabbing for handholds and hauling himself up, lurching from tree to boulder to depression—whatever he could find for cover. Bullets riddled the rock below him, but he had moved out of range. Not looking back, he made a mad dash for the top, propelled by a vision of the mountain collapsing beneath him.

"Jack, over here!" Brian's words, low and urgent, beckoned him. He moved toward them and found the teenager, Andrea and Ian huddled in the lee of the broken tower from an old mining tram.

"We've got to get out of here." Jack grabbed Andrea's arm and pulled her forward. "Move! Now!"

His lungs burned and the ache in his leg sent shock waves of pain through him with every step, but he ignored the pain, willing himself to focus on nothing but survival and protecting the people in his care. They had reached a false summit and were running along a high plateau when the ground shook beneath them. Brian stumbled and fell, and Andrea screamed. Jack launched himself on top of her and together they fell.

Chapter Fifteen

Andrea broke her fall with her hands and knees and rolled to bring Ian between her and Jack. The first shock wave was followed by a second. Then everything stilled, the silence like a roaring wind in her ears.

"What happened?" she asked, the words half-sobbed.

Brian crawled over to them. "Are you okay?" she asked.

"The snow cushioned our fall. I'm okay." He looked at Jack. "Was that a bomb?"

"I used some of the plastic explosives we found," he said.

"You built a bomb?" She gaped at him.

"Something like that," he said. "It was the only thing I could think of."

"That should slow them down," Brian said.

"Slow them down, but it may not stop them." Jack sat up. "We've got to get out of here."

"I don't even know where 'here' is," Andrea said. "Or where we can go that's safe."

"Now is when we need a smartphone," Brian said. "With GPS and a map. Do you think they have an app that would help us avoid crazed terrorist killers?"

"You mean like a video game?" Ian asked.

"Uh, yeah. Just like a video game." He reached into the pocket of his jeans. "I've got a little piece of chocolate left," he said. "Do you want it, Ian?"

"Yeah!" The boy reached for the treat.

"Thanks," Andrea said. Brian had a good head on his shoulders, and he was holding up pretty well, considering the circumstances.

"So what do we do now?" Brian asked.

Jack looked up at the tram tower. "Where do you think this goes?" he asked. "I mean, where do you think it went when it was in working order?"

"I guess down the mountain to the river or a road or a railroad, or to a mill or something where they processed the ore," Brian said.

Jack kicked at a rusted length of iron cable that lay at the base of the tower. "There are probably more of these towers, then," he said.

"Yeah," Brian said. "I see them all the time when I'm out hiking. And pieces of cable, too. When they abandoned the mines and mills, they left all this stuff up here. Some of the iron stuff was collected and sold as scrap during World War II, but most of it is still lying around."

"Then we'll follow the tramline as far as we can," Jack said. "When we get to the end, hopefully we'll find our way back to civilization."

Andrea suppressed a moan. Stumbling down a mountain in the darkness, carrying a child who grew heavier by the minute, seemed an impossible task. "I don't think I can do it," she said.

Jack knelt beside her. "You can do it," he said. "You're strong. And the longer we stay on the move, the less the chance that those murderers will find us."

"Maybe none of them are left," she said. "After that explosion…"

"Duane Braeswood has the money and the resources to keep hunting us. If he doesn't hear from this bunch when they're supposed to check in, he'll send more men. Another helicopter. Weapons. We can't assume he's going to stop until we know we're safe."

She shuddered, remembering the masked faces and cruel voices of the five men who had captured her. Their casual talk of murdering Ian and Brian, not to mention Jack, made her sick to her stomach.

But the memory of their words also made her angry. She struggled to her feet. "All right," she said. "I'll keep going." If Jack wasn't ready to surrender, then neither was she.

AFTER THREE HOURS of walking steadily downhill, the group came to a plateau scattered with rusting metal ruins. Moonlight cast eerie shadows over twisted cables and rusting pulleys, broken timbers and the shell of an old boiler rising from the snow. "This must have been where they processed the ore from the mine," Jack said. He leaned on the tree branch he had cut several miles back to use as a crutch. The fact that he had resorted to using such an aid told Andrea how much his leg must be paining him.

Brian, a sleeping Ian in his arms, joined them. The two men had taken turns carrying Ian most of the way, after Andrea had almost dropped him from exhaustion. As it was, she was pretty sure she could have been perfectly cast as an extra in the latest zombie film. She'd willed herself for the last hour to stop thinking about anything but putting one foot in front of the other. "I took a geology course last semester and we visited a site like this," Brian said. "The professor said they hauled away most of the stamp mills to other locations when the mines played out. I guess they were worth enough money to make moving them a good idea." He looked around them. "But there should be a road around here somewhere. They would have hauled the processed ore by wagon or train to someplace else."

Andrea put her hand on Jack's arm. "We can look for the road in the morning," she said. "Right now we've got to stop and rest."

Brian lowered Ian to the ground, then sat beside him. "You could try to call for help again," he said.

Several times during their trek down the mountain, Jack had tried to telephone his boss but had been unable to get a strong enough signal for the call to go through.

He took the phone from his pocket and switched it on. After a few seconds, he shook his head. "No signal," he said.

He looked exhausted, deep lines of weariness and pain etched on either side of his mouth and around his eyes. Andrea wanted to go to him and hold him, but she knew he would misinterpret the gesture as her needing comfort from him.

"Let's move to the woods over there." He gestured toward the thick growth of forest on the edge of the plateau. "I don't like being out in the open like this."

"You're right." Andrea hugged her arms across her chest. She had a feeling it would be a long time before she could stand in the open without feeling like a target.

Once in the woods, they settled down with their backs against tree trunks or stretched on the ground. Though the cold seeped into them, they were out of the wind. If they stayed close together under the blankets, they should be all right. Andrea settled beside Jack. "There's probably ibuprofen in the first-aid kit in that pack." Until this moment, she had forgotten about the medical supplies in the pack Jack had found at the fishing camp.

"I took it a couple of hours ago," he said. "When we stopped at that creek to get water."

"Did it help?"

"Some."

"Liar."

The corners of his mouth tugged up and that attempt at a smile made her heart feel lighter. "What's going to happen when we get out of here?" she asked. She ought to try to sleep, and let him rest as well, but the question had been worrying at her for most of the last day. Exhaustion or the darkness or maybe simply desperation had given her the courage to ask it.

"I hope the evidence we've collected and whatever we find at the camp and the mine will help us to stop these people and bring them to justice," he said.

Of course. He had thought of his job first. Of the case. "I meant, what is going to happen with us?" she asked.

He turned his head toward her. "I want to keep seeing you," he said.

"If you solve the case, you won't stay in Durango."

"Maybe not. But they have these things called planes."

"I don't want a part-time relationship," she said. She had already had one of those, considering how much of Preston's focus had been on his work and not his home life. Even when he was with her and Ian, she could tell he was thinking about the job.

He let out a long breath. "I don't know what to tell you," he said. "I want to be with you and Ian.

Can't you just have faith that we'll find a way to work this out?"

She needed more from him than wishful thinking and maybes. She needed—what—a commitment? From a man she had known only a few days? "You're right," she said. "This isn't the best time to be discussing this. We'll have plenty of time later." She patted his knee, then stood and joined Ian and Brian a few feet away. Ian still felt feverish and his lethargy during the hike down the mountain worried her. She needed to focus on her son instead of worrying about a man who could leave her life as quickly as he had entered it.

Andrea was sleeping when a low, throbbing noise entered her dreams. She pulled the blanket, which she was sharing with Ian, more tightly around her and willed herself back to dreamland. Maybe this was a dream, too, or the beginning of a nightmare.

Jack shook her. "Get up," he said. "Someone's coming."

"Is that another helicopter?" Brian asked. He sat up and looked around.

"Come on," Jack said. "Get up and bring everything with you. Whoever it is probably doesn't know we're here yet."

"How long have we been here?" she asked.

"A couple of hours," Jack said. "It will be dawn soon."

Andrea would have thought she was too exhausted to take another step, but fear propelled her forward once more. She didn't know if Ian even woke as she picked him up. She followed Jack and Brian farther into the woods.

"How did they find us?" Brian asked.

"They probably figured out we would follow the tramline," Jack said. "It was the most direct route off the mountain. I knew we were taking a risk using it, but any other course in the dark seemed too dangerous."

"Jack, I can't keep running through the woods like this," Andrea said. "I'm sorry, but I can't. And neither can Ian."

"Neither can any of us." He positioned himself behind a tree. "Do you still have the gun I gave you?" he asked.

"Yes." The hard pistol dug into the small of her back, though in her exhaustion, the discomfort hadn't been enough to keep her from sleeping.

"Do you think you can shoot it?"

"Yes, of course," she said. Hadn't they had this conversation once already?

"Would you kill a man to protect Ian?"

"Yes." She swallowed hard at the idea, but she knew she meant it. She would do anything to protect her son.

"Then find cover and be ready to shoot if anyone comes through the woods toward us. They won't be expecting us and if we're lucky and there aren't too many of them, we can pick them off before they get to us."

"What do you want me to do?" Brian asked.

"Take Ian and go about a hundred yards back. If we go down, you run, as far and as fast as you can. We'll try to distract them long enough for you to get away."

Andrea drew the gun and moved to stand behind a tree about twenty yards from Jack. She couldn't believe this was happening—that she was about to engage in a shoot-out in the woods, in the middle of the night, with killers. She was an ordinary woman—a mother and a psychologist. Nothing in her training had prepared her for this.

She heard Brian move away. She didn't look back, afraid she might cry if she saw Ian leaving her. Instead, she gripped the gun more tightly and tried to focus on the glow of light coming from the clearing they had just left. The throb of the helicopter rose until it was too loud to talk over. Light pierced the trees, and then the engine slowed but didn't die altogether. A door slammed. She imagined the killers piling out, in their battle gear, weapons ready. How many of them were there? Jack had said the helicopter would hold six people in addition to the pilot. How many men had died in the explosion on the mountain? Or had they brought in reinforcements, fresh troops who weren't exhausted by a trek up and down mountains?

"Agent Jack Prescott!" The words had the hollow, echoing sound of a command issued through a bullhorn.

Jack stiffened but made no response.

"This is Captain A. J. Lansing of the La Plata County Sheriff's Department SWAT. Special Agent Ted Blessing contacted us. We understand you have a woman and a child and another young man with you. If you can hear us, please acknowledge."

Jack relaxed. "We're here!" he shouted. "We're coming out!"

Andrea's first sight of their rescuers was of a man dressed in black-and-olive fatigues with a large German shepherd by his side. Ian gave an exclamation of surprise and leaned forward to gape at the dog. Andrea took her son from Brian and followed Jack into the clearing. The helicopter had shut down, making it easier to talk. "Dr. McNeil," the man greeted her. "I'm Alan Lansing. And this must be Ian."

"What's your dog's name?" Ian asked.

"This is Bella." At the sound of her name, Bella wagged her tail back and forth.

Two other SWAT team members joined them. "How did you find us?" Jack asked.

"We located you using the ping on your phone."

"Do we need to radio ahead for a medic?" one of the officers asked, eyeing Jack's makeshift crutch.

"I'm fine." Jack tossed the stick aside.

Andrea wanted to protest that he obviously wasn't

fine—that none of them were. But Jack probably didn't need a medic right away, and he wouldn't appreciate her embarrassing him in front of another law enforcement officer.

"We've got food and water and blankets in the chopper," Lansing said. "Let's get loaded up and get you folks home."

They filed to the helicopter and were waiting to climb in when a burst of gunfire tore through the area.

Chapter Sixteen

Bullets rang against the side of the helicopter and one of the SWAT members collapsed. Andrea screamed. Then she and Ian were shoved to the ground. Jack slammed his body into theirs and rolled them beneath the chopper. He lay on top of them, his weight crushing yet reassuring. Ian began to cry. "Shh. It's going to be okay." Andrea tried to comfort him. The shooting had stopped, but the explosions still echoed in her ears. Her heart hammered as if she'd run up a mountain, and Jack's weight on top of her made it difficult to breathe.

"Where are the others?" she whispered, afraid the shooter might hear.

"Brian is inside the chopper with the pilot," Jack said. "Lansing and the dog took cover behind some rocks. I don't know where the third man is."

The sun was just breaking over the horizon and in the still-faint pinkish light, she could make out a narrow section of the clearing in front of the chopper. The officer who had been shot lay facedown in the snow, very still. Too still. She hoped Ian couldn't see him.

"Where is the shooter?" she asked.

"On the west side of the clearing. He must have been following us. He came up the same trail we did." He shifted, taking some of his weight from her. "I'm going to try to get a better look at him."

"No." She clutched at his wrist. "It's too danger-ous."

"I won't do anything stupid." He moved until he lay on the ground facing her. "I've got too much to live for to take foolish risks, but I've got to do whatever I can to end this." He kissed her, hard and fierce. She wanted to cling to him, to beg him not to leave her. But she knew he wasn't the type of man who would stand by and let others be hurt while he had the power to prevent it. That was one of the things she loved about him.

"Come back to me," she whispered, but he had already moved away.

JACK CROUCHED BEHIND the wheel strut of the helicop-ter and scanned the edge of the woods, searching for the shooter. The sun rising behind him cast a feeble light over the clearing, the shadow of the helicopter stretching out on the ground directly in front of him. Only one gun had fired on the group, so he thought it possible there was only one man—perhaps the only survivor of the bomb Jack had launched.

Movement to Jack's right distracted him. He shifted slightly and recognized Captain Lansing slumped behind a boulder. Blood stained the shoulder of his uniform, and the German shepherd, Bella, lay curled against him. The dog watched Jack, ears up and eyes alert, but didn't move.

Jack needed to draw out the shooter. He didn't want to give the man enough time to circle around behind them. Taking careful aim, he fired at the point he thought the shots had emanated from.

The shooter responded with another blast of gunfire, bullets blasting chunks of fiberglass from the side of the helicopter. Ian began to wail and the gunfire shifted, hitting the ground right in front of where Andrea and Ian lay. The thought of either one of them being hit was a physical pain gripping Jack's chest. "Come out where I can see you, you coward!" he shouted.

The only response was gunfire, but not from the shooter. Captain Lansing had raised himself up enough to fire his own weapon toward the shooter. A muffled cry indicated that—maybe—the captain had found his target.

Lansing caught Jack's eye and jerked his head toward the woods behind the chopper. Jack nodded. If he made the cover of the trees, he could slip around behind the shooter. If Lansing kept the man's attention focused on him, Jack would have a good chance of getting close without being detected.

Lansing opened fire again and Jack ran, keeping his body low and ignoring the pain in his thigh. He stopped a few yards into the trees to catch his breath and listen. The shooter had returned fire again. As far as Jack could tell, the man hadn't changed locations.

He shifted his gaze to the helicopter. The sun had almost completely risen now, light glinting off the chopper's drooping blades. He couldn't see Andrea and Ian from here, but he knew they were under there. As long as he and Lansing kept the shooter busy, the man wouldn't be able to move in closer and get a clear shot at Andrea and the others.

Slowly, stealthily, Jack crept from tree to tree. Every few minutes a fresh burst of gunfire alerted him to the gunman's location. Then, as he reached the west side of the clearing, a movement ahead caught his eye. A darker shadow shifted between the tree trunks. Jack took a step toward it and a twig snapped beneath his boot. The shadowy figure whirled, gun raised. Jack dived behind a tree.

The shooter shifted again, perhaps to get a better look at Jack. A shaft of light cut between the trees, spotlighting the side of the man's face before he ducked behind the tree trunk once more.

But that one glimpse had been enough to stop Jack's breath. A dizzying flood of emotion and memory washed over him: suddenly, he was standing on the front deck of the mountain home that had been rented by the suspected ringleader of the terrorist cell. Search Team Seven had a warrant to search the property and plant listening devices they would use to gather evidence to make their case against Duane Braeswood and the people with him in the house. Gus Mathers stood in the yard a few feet below Jack, tracing a phone line around the side of the house.

Then a man stepped out from behind a tree and shot Gus. Jack saw his friend fall, then turned to look at the shooter. Their eyes met, and the man raised his rifle to fire at Jack. Jack dived to the side so that, though the bullets put him in the hospital for weeks, he didn't die. The image of the man's face shimmered in his mind, as crystal clear and unforgettable as his own reflection.

"You!" Jack hadn't even realized he had spoken out loud, but the single word brought him back to the present—and to the people who needed his protection now. He stared at the man, who had peered from behind the tree at his shout. "You killed my friend," Jack said—a statement, not an accusation.

"And I will kill you," the man said, and raised his weapon.

But Jack had already raised his pistol. He fired once…twice…and the man slumped to the ground, his gun sliding across the snow and coming to rest against another tree a few feet away.

Jack didn't know how long he stood over the body, the pistol in his hand, before Andrea joined him.

"Jack?" She spoke softly, concern and caution shaping her expression.

He holstered his weapon and turned to her. "He's the man who shot Gus," he said. "I remembered."

"I'm glad he didn't shoot you." She didn't quite smile, but it was enough to shatter the last brittle barrier of reserve within him. He held out his arms and she came to him. They comforted each other for a long moment as the sun rose higher in the sky and the helicopter's engines roared to life.

"Where's Ian?" he asked after a while.

"He's in the helicopter with Brian and the others. Captain Lansing is shot, but Corporal Scott thinks he's going to be okay." Her expression saddened. "Sergeant Rialto wasn't so lucky." She pressed her forehead to his chest. "Jack, I was so afraid."

"Yeah." He patted her back. "I was afraid, too. But we're okay now. We're all okay."

She looked up at him, some inner strength illuminating her face despite the weariness. "Let's go home now," she said.

He put his arm around her. "Yeah. Let's go home."

"I CAN'T BELIEVE you went through all of that and you still look so...so normal!" Chelsea pressed her hand against her chest and studied Andrea across the kitchen table, two days after her return home. "It's like something out of a movie or something."

"It's definitely not something I want to relive."

Andrea sipped her coffee. "I'm glad it's over and I'm ready for life to get back to normal."

"Ian seems to be doing okay." Chelsea turned toward the living room and Andrea followed her gaze to where Ian was playing with baby Charlotte.

"He's doing great," she said. Though Ian had slept with her their first night home, that had been as much for her benefit as her son's and now he was back in his regular routine—although he had asked about Jack several times during the past two days.

"What about Jack?" Chelsea asked. "Have you heard from him?"

"He called and left a message while I was at work yesterday—just checking to see how we were doing." No great declarations of love or even an invitation to dinner. *I wanted to make sure you and Ian are okay. It's been crazy busy here, but you've been on my mind.* The kind of message any friend might leave.

"Are you going to see him again?" Chelsea asked.

"I don't know." She pushed the coffee cup away. "I'm not sure that's a good idea."

"What do you mean? Did something happen out there that changed your mind about him?"

"I wasn't aware that I'd made up my mind about him before," Andrea said. "If you recall, before this whole thing happened, we had only just met."

Chelsea waved this notion away. "Call me a romantic, but the first time I saw you two together, I could tell something clicked. You seemed perfect together. Did anything that happened to you while you were running around in the woods make you think otherwise?"

A kaleidoscope of memories played through her mind: Jack playing with Ian on the floor of the cabin, Jack making love to her with such exquisite tenderness and passion, Jack protecting her with his own body as a terrorist shot at them. Every image proved that he was a man of strength and character, capable of great emotion and caring.

"Jack has a very dangerous job," she said, choosing her words carefully. "One that requires a lot of his time and attention. The things that happened to us after those men kidnapped Ian—that kind of thing happens to Jack all the time. I think Ian and I need a little more stability in our lives."

"Maybe you do." Chelsea leaned forward and covered Andrea's hand with her own. "Or maybe you need a man who will go to the ends of the earth to protect you with everything he has. I know after what happened with Preston, getting anywhere near a law enforcement officer has to be scary, but tell the truth—in the three years you've been a widow, has any other man come even close to lighting you up the way Jack does?"

"Are you saying I have a thing for dangerous men?"

Chelsea sat back, smiling. "Maybe you do. Or maybe they have a thing for you."

The doorbell rang and Ian jumped up. "I'll get it!" he shouted.

"Ian, remember what I told you about opening the door to strangers." Andrea hurried after her son, Chelsea behind her.

"Hello, Andrea."

By the time the women made it to the door, Jack was standing just inside with Ian.

As a psychologist, Andrea was familiar with all the physical manifestations of attraction—pounding heart, wobbly knees and light-headedness, for example. Clearly, her body was determined to remind her of the attraction she felt for Jack by manifesting every symptom in the book. "Hello, Jack." Shaking, breathy voice—check.

"I'll just leave you two alone to talk." Chelsea took Ian's hand. "Come on, Ian. Let's take Charlotte outside to play for a little bit."

"But I want to see Jack," Ian wailed.

"I promise to come see you when I'm done talking to your mom," Jack said. "I brought that oil for your tricycle and I'll need you to help me work on it."

"We could work on it now," Ian said.

"Let me talk to your mom first."

"Okay," he relented.

By the time they were alone, Andrea felt in more control of her emotions. "How are you doing, Jack?" she asked.

He took a step toward her, moving a little more

stiffly than he had when they first met. "Are you asking as my therapist or as my friend?"

She fought the urge to back up. "Both," she said.

"My physical therapist lectured me on all the damage I've done by not staying off my leg and taking it easy, but she says I'll recover in time. My boss has agreed to give me a desk job for a while, since I managed to get into so much trouble while I was on leave. As for the rest…" He shrugged. "I'm grateful I remembered Gus's killer. I hated having that gap in my memory. It made me doubt myself—as a friend and as an agent with a job to do."

"So you have closure." She clasped her hands tightly in front of her to keep from reaching out to him. Did she and Ian and everything that had happened between them not count with "the rest"?

"His name was Roland Chambers. He was suspected of being Duane Braeswood's second in command. Taking him out put one more chink in the organization."

"He's out of your life for good now," she said. "You can move on with the work you love."

"I guess so. We've confirmed the backpack I found in the mine definitely belonged to Mark Renfro. We still don't know where he is or if he's even alive, but it gives us a lead to follow. We're still looking for the rest of the group, but we hope the evidence we've collected at the mine and at the fishing camp will eventually lead us to them."

"How's Brian?" she asked. "I want to get his contact information and keep in touch with him."

"He'd like that. He's back in Boulder right now. We were able to contact his dad and he flew in from Iceland yesterday. He hadn't taken the threats against his son seriously. He thought they were some kind of fraternity prank or something and was too engrossed in his work to pay attention. I think this was a real wake-up call for him. He's talking about taking Brian back to Iceland with him."

"I guess this is the kind of thing that would shake up anyone," she said.

"How are you and Ian doing?" he asked.

"Ian is great. I guess it's true about little kids—they're very resilient. Right now all he cares about is counting down the days until Christmas. But I've made an appointment for him with a friend of mine who specializes in children's therapy, just to make sure there's no lingering concerns."

"And you?"

She pressed her lips together, choosing her words carefully. "What happened shook me up a little," she said. "I…I know we wouldn't have made it without you."

He took another step toward her, until she could feel the heat of him and see the rise and fall of his chest as he breathed. "There's something you need to know," he said.

She forced herself to meet his eyes, and the searching look he gave her made her breath catch.

She pressed her lips together, afraid to speak, to break the spell between them.

"When I faced that shooter in the woods, it wasn't about Gus or the job or protecting myself or anything like that. It wasn't even about revenge. All I wanted was to protect you. You and Ian. You were the only things that mattered. The only things that still matter."

"Oh, Jack." She pressed her fingers to her lips, a sob catching in her throat. He gathered her close and she relaxed against him, unable to hold back anymore.

He kissed the top of her head, his hands caressing her back. "I love you," he said. "You know that, don't you?"

She nodded. "Yes. I love you, too. I know we just met, but…"

"But it's right. I'm as certain of that as…as I am that I would never forget your face." He pulled back enough to smile at her and she returned the expression, happiness filling her up like light.

"What about your job?" she asked.

"What about it?"

"You won't be in Durango forever."

"I could be," he said. "The Bureau's resident agency here in Durango has an opening."

"What about your case?"

"I can stay with the team until they leave here, then transfer to the resident agency."

She clutched his shirt front. "You'd do that for me?"

"I told you. You and Ian are what matter most to me now." He cradled her head in his hand and kissed her. The kiss was as familiar and welcome as the taste of sweet chocolate and as intoxicating as an exotic liqueur. This was what life with Jack would bring her—his steadfast love and protection along with an electric dose of the unexpected. As much as she claimed to crave the ordinary and sedate, she knew Chelsea had been right. Jack's courage and willingness to face danger, to right wrongs, attracted her every bit as much as his muscular shoulders and tenderness toward Ian.

"Jack!"

Andrea's whole body hummed with the effect of that kiss when Jack raised his head to look at Ian. "What is it, Ian?"

"Are you staying?"

Jack looked at Andrea, who nodded. "I'm staying, buddy," Jack said.

"Then do you think, pretty soon, that you could teach me to ride a big bike? I asked Santa to bring me one for Christmas."

Jack released her and knelt in front of her son. "I hope I can teach you that, and a lot of other things," he said.

"Good." Ian threw his arms around Jack's neck and hugged him tightly. Andrea knelt to join in the embrace.

"The three of us are going to be a family now," she said. "Would you like that?"

"Uh-huh." He stepped back to regard them both solemnly. "Does this mean we can get a dog?"

"We'll have to talk about that later." Jack stood and helped Andrea up beside him. He put his arm around her and looked at Ian. "What do you think about me marrying your mother?"

Ian studied them a moment. "I guess that would be okay." He turned and headed out of the room. "I'll get my trike out of the garage. You can meet me out there."

Jack laughed. "I guess you're right," he said. "Nothing fazes him."

"Are you sure you're ready for this?" Andrea asked.

"More than ready." He began kissing her again and she wrapped herself around him. Ian and his trike would clearly have to wait a few minutes longer.

* * * * *

Cindi Myers's miniseries
THE MEN OF SEARCH TEAM SEVEN
continues next month with PHD PROTECTOR.
Look for it wherever
Harlequin Intrigue books are sold!

INTRIGUE

Available November 22, 2016

#1677 CARDWELL CHRISTMAS CRIME SCENE
Cardwell Cousins • by B.J. Daniels
Dee Anna Justice doesn't know what to make of private investigator Beau Tanner and the Cardwell family, who seem ready to welcome her with open arms. Her convict father says she needs to be protected from a deadly threat—but can she bring down her walls and let Beau in?

#1678 INVESTIGATING CHRISTMAS
Colby Agency: Family Secrets
by Debra Webb & Regan Black
Lucy Gaines walked away from sexy billionaire Rush Grayson before—the man who has it all seems to have no capacity for love. But when Lucy's sister and nephew are kidnapped, Rush is the only one who can save them and bring her family home for Christmas.

#1679 KANSAS CITY COUNTDOWN
The Precinct: Bachelors in Blue • by Julie Miller
Detective Keir Watson has seventy-two hours to identify the man terrorizing attorney Kenna Parker. Her amnesia makes identifying her stalker difficult. But trusting his growing feelings for the older woman? Impossible.

#1680 PHD PROTECTOR
The Men of Search Team Seven • by Cindi Myers
Nuclear scientist Mark Renfro has been kidnapped by a terrorist cell planning to detonate a nuclear bomb. On the verge of hopelessness, he meets Erin Daniels, the stepdaughter of his captor, whose life is also on the line. Only by working together can they escape, and the clock is ticking...

#1681 OVERWHELMING FORCE
Omega Sector: Critical Response • by Janie Crouch
Joe Matarazzo is the best hostage negotiator Omega Sector has ever seen. But when his ex-lover, lawyer Laura Birchwood, is in a stalker's sights, the situation may be more than even he can handle.

#1682 MOUNTAIN SHELTER
by Cassie Miles
When an international assassin targets neurosurgeon Jayne Shackleford, it's up to Dylan Simmons to keep her safe. A bodyguard and tech genius, Dylan understands Jayne's emotional isolation, and his safe house in the mountains just might have her letting down her defenses.

DJ Justice opened the door to her apartment and froze.
Nothing looked out of place and yet she took a step back.
Her gaze went to the lock. There were scratches around
the keyhole. The lock set was one of the first things she'd
replaced when she'd rented the apartment.

She eased her hand into the large leather hobo bag that
she always carried. Her palm fit smoothly around the grip
of the weapon, loaded and ready to fire, as she slowly
pushed open the door.

The apartment was small and sparsely furnished. She
never stayed anywhere long, so she collected nothing of
value that couldn't fit into one suitcase. Spending years
on the run as a child, she'd had to leave places in the
middle of the night with only minutes to pack.

But that had changed over the past few years. She'd
just begun to feel...safe. She liked her job, felt content
here. She should have known it couldn't last.

The door creaked open at the touch of her finger, and she quickly scanned the living area. Moving deeper into the apartment, she stepped to the open bathroom door and glanced in. Nothing amiss. At a glance she could see the bathtub, sink and toilet as well as the mirror on the medicine cabinet. The shower door was clear glass. Nothing behind it.

That left just the bedroom. As she stepped soundlessly toward it, she wanted to be wrong. And yet she knew someone had been here. But why break in unless he or she planned to take something?

Or leave something?

Like the time she'd found the bloody hatchet on the fire escape right outside her window when she was eleven. That message had been for her father, the blood from a chicken, he'd told her. Or maybe it hadn't even been blood, he'd said. As if she hadn't seen his fear. As if they hadn't thrown everything they owned into suitcases and escaped in the middle of the night.

She moved to the open bedroom door. The room was small enough that there was sufficient room only for a bed and a simple nightstand with one shelf. The book she'd been reading the night before was on the nightstand, nothing else.

The double bed was made—just as she'd left it.

She started to turn away when she caught a glimmer of something out of the corner of her eye.

Don't miss CARDWELL CHRISTMAS CRIME SCENE by B.J. Daniels, available December 2016 wherever Harlequin® Intrigue books and ebooks are sold.

www.Harlequin.com

EXCLUSIVE
Limited Time Offer

$1.⁰⁰ OFF

New York Times Bestselling Author

B.J. DANIELS

Protecting her life will mean betraying her trust…

HONOR BOUND

Available October 18, 2016.
Pick up your copy today!

NEW YORK TIMES
Bestselling Author

B.J. DANIELS

"B.J. Daniels is at the top of her game… The perfect blend of hot romance and thrilling suspense."
—New York Times bestselling author
ALLISON BRENNAN

HONOR BOUND

THE
MONTANA HAMILTONS

$7.99 U.S./$9.99 CAN.

HQN™

$1.⁰⁰ OFF the purchase price of HONOR BOUND by B.J. Daniels.

Offer valid from October 18, 2016, to November 30, 2016.
Redeemable at participating retail outlets. Not redeemable at Barnes & Noble.
Limit one coupon per purchase. Valid in the U.S.A. and Canada only.

52613975

5 65373 00076 2   (8100)0 12189

® and ™ are trademarks owned and used by the trademark owner and/or its licensee.

© 2016 Harlequin Enterprises Limited

PHCOUPBJD1116

THE WORLD IS BETTER WITH

Romance

Harlequin has everything from contemporary, passionate and heartwarming to suspenseful and inspirational stories.

Whatever your mood, we have romance when you need it, wherever you are!

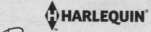

HARLEQUIN®

A *Romance* FOR EVERY MOOD™

www.Harlequin.com

#RomanceWhenYouNeedIt

HSHMYBPA2016